TWIN RIDGES HOME SERVICE

The Captives of Kaag

You unsheathe the sun-sword and hold it before your face. At once a golden halo of flames bursts from its polished blade, causing the Helghast to shriek in alarm as it recognizes the power you wield. It breaks off its advance and staggers back towards the bridge, desperate to flee its nemesis. Determinedly you chase after this evil being and, as it reaches the draw-bridge, you come within a sword's length of its spine.

"Die, foul spawn!" you cry, and with one fell sweep of your arm, you cleave the demonic creature cleanly in two . . .

Joe Dever was born in 1956 at Woodford Bridge in the U.K. After he left college, he became a professional musician, working in studios in Europe and America. While working in Los Angeles in 1977, he discovered a game called "Dungeons and Dragons" and was soon an enthusiastic player. Five years later he won the Advanced Dungeons and Dragons Championship in the U.S., where he was the only British competitor. The Lone Wolf adventures are the culmination of many years of developing the world of Magnamund. They are printed in several languages and are sold all over the world.

W9-AAU-210

BOOK 14
The Captives of Kaag

Joe Dever
Illustrated by Brian Williams

Abridged Edition

TWIN RIDGES HOME STUDY

BERKLEY BOOKS, NEW YORK

This role-playing novel was published
in an expanded form in the United Kingdom.

THE CAPTIVES OF KAAG

A Berkley Book / published by arrangement with
Red Fox, Random Century Ltd.

PRINTING HISTORY
Red Fox Book edition published 1991
Berkley abridged edition / June 1992

ISBN: 0-425-13304-4

A BERKLEY BOOK ® TM 757,375
Berkley Books are published by The Berkley Publishing Group,
200 Madison Avenue, New York, New York 10016.
The name "BERKLEY" and the "B" logo are trademarks belonging to
Berkley Publishing Corporation.

PRINTED IN THE UNITED STATES OF AMERICA

10 9 8 7 6 5 4 3 2

*To Mike, Jeannie
and Megan*

GRAND MASTER DISCIPLINES   NOTES

1	Grand Weapon Mastery
2	Grand Hunting
3	Grand Invisibility
4	Magi-Magic
5	5th Grand Master Discipline if you have completed 1 Grand Master adventure successfully

BACKPACK (max. 10 articles)	MEALS
1 Map	2
2 Blue Pills	
3 Meal	
4 Meal	
5 Sack of silver	—3 EP if no Meal available when instructed to eat.
6 Key	BELT POUCH Containing Gold Crowns (50 maximum)
7 Silver bowl	
8	50
9	Crowns
10	

CS = COMBAT SKILL   EP = ENDURANCE POINTS

ACTION CHART

COMBAT SKILL	ENDURANCE POINTS
33 49	48 42
	0 = dead

COMBAT RECORD

ENDURANCE POINTS		ENDURANCE POINTS
LONE WOLF	COMBAT RATIO	ENEMY
LONE WOLF	COMBAT RATIO	ENEMY
LONE WOLF	COMBAT RATIO	ENEMY
LONE WOLF	COMBAT RATIO	ENEMY
LONE WOLF	COMBAT RATIO	ENEMY
GRAND MASTER RANK		

SPECIAL ITEMS LIST

DESCRIPTION	KNOWN EFFECTS

WEAPONS LIST

WEAPONS (maximum 2 Weapons)
1   Silverbow   + 8.5
2   Sommerswerd   + 10.5
If holding Weapon and appropriate Grand Weaponmastery in combat + 5CS

GRAND WEAPONMASTERY CHECKLIST

DAGGER		SPEAR	
MACE		SHORT SWORD	
WARHAMMER		BOW	✓
AXE		SWORD	✓
QUARTERSTAFF		BROADSWORD	✓

QUIVER & ARROWS

Quiver	No. of arrows carried
YES/NO	30

THE STORY SO FAR ...

You are Grand Master Lone Wolf, last of the Kai Lords of Sommerlund and sole survivor of a massacre that wiped out the First Order of your elite warrior caste.

It is the year MS 5075 and twenty-five years have passed since your brave kinsmen perished at the hands of the Dark-lords of Helgedad. These champions of evil, who were sent forth by Naar, the King of the Darkness, to destroy the fertile world of Magnamund, have themselves since been de-stroyed. You vowed to avenge the murder of the Kai and you kept your pledge, for it was you who brought about their downfall when alone you infiltrated their foul domain—the Darklands—and caused the destruction of their leader, Archlord Gnaag, and the seat of his power that was the infernal city of Helgedad.

In the wake of their destruction, chaos befell the Darkland armies who, until then, had been poised to conquer all of northern Magnamund. Some factions which comprised this huge army, most notably the barbaric Drakkarim, began to fight with the others for control. This disorder quickly esca-lated into an all-out civil war, which allowed the freestate armies of Magnamund time in which to recover and launch a counter-offensive. Skillfully their commanders exploited

1

the chaos and secured a swift and total victory over an enemy far superior in numbers.

For five years now peace has reigned in Sommerlund. Under your direction, the once-ruined monastery of the Kai has been thoroughly rebuilt and restored to its former glory, and the task of teaching a Second Order of Kai warriors the skills and proud traditions of your ancestors is also well underway. The new generation of Kai recruits, all of whom were born during the era of war against the Darklords, possesses latent Kai skills and all show exceptional promise. These skills will be nurtured and honed to perfection during their time at the monastery so that they may teach and inspire future generations, thereby ensuring the continued security of your homeland in future years.

Your attainment of the rank of Kai Grand Master brought with it great rewards. Some, such as the restoration of the Kai and the undying gratitude of your fellow Sommlending, could have been anticipated. Yet there have also been rewards which you could not possibly have foreseen. The discovery that within you lay the potential to develop Kai Disciplines beyond those of the Magnakai, which, until now, were thought to be the ultimate that a Kai Master could aspire to, was truly a revelation. Your discovery has inspired you to set out upon a new and previously unknown path in search of the wisdom and power that no Kai lord before you has ever possessed. In the name of your creator, the God Kai, and for the greater glory of Sommerlund and the Goddess Ishir, you have vowed to reach the very pinnacle of Kai perfection—to attain all of the Grand Master Disciplines and become the first Kai Supreme Master.

With diligence and determination you set about the restoration of the Kai monastery and organized the training of the Second Order recruits. Your efforts were soon rewarded and, within the space of two short years, the first raw recruits had graduated to become a cadre of gifted Kai Masters who,

2

in turn, were able to commence the teaching of their skills to subsequent intakes of Kai novices. Readily the Kai Masters rose to their new-found responsibilities, leaving you free to devote more of your time to the pursuit and perfection of the Grand Master Disciplines.

During this period you also received expert tutelage in the ways of magic from two of your most trusted friends and advisors: Guildmaster Banedon, leader of the Brotherhood of the Crystal Star, and Lord Rimoah, speaker for the High Council of the Elder Magi.

In the deepest subterranean level of the monastery, one hundred feet below the Tower of the Sun, you ordered the excavation and construction of a special vault. In this magnificent chamber wrought of granite and gold, you placed the seven Lorestones of Nyxator, the gems of Kai power that you had recovered during your quest for the Magnakai. It was here, bathed in the golden light of those radiant gems, that you spent countless hours in pursuit of perfection. Sometimes alone, sometimes in the company of your two able advisors—Banedon and Rimoah—you worked hard to develop your innate Grand Master Disciplines, and grasp the fundamental secrets of Left-handed and Old Kingdom magic. During this time you noticed many remarkable changes taking place within your body: you became physically and mentally stronger, your five primary senses sharpened beyond all that you had experienced before, and, perhaps most remarkably, your body began to age at a much slower rate. Now, for every five years that elapse you age but one year.

At this time many changes were occurring beyond the borders of Sommerlund. In the regions to the northeast of Magador and the Maakengorge, the Elder Magi of Dessi and the Herbwardens of Bautar were working together in an effort to restore the dusty volcanic wasteland to its former fertile state. It was the first tentative step towards the reclamation of all the Darklands. However, their progress was painfully slow and both parties were resigned to the fact that their efforts to undo the damage caused by the Darklords would take not years but centuries to complete.

In the far west, the Drakkarim had retreated to their homelands and were engaged in a bloody war against the Lencians. Much of Nyras had been reclaimed by the armies of King Sarnac, the Lencian commander, and his flag now flew over territory which, two thousand years ago, had once been part of Lencia.

Following the destruction of the Darklords of Helgedad, the Giaks, the most prolific in number of all of Gnaag's troops, fled into the Darklands and sought refuge in the gigantic city-fortresses of Nadgazad, Aarnak, Gournen and Kaag. Within each of these hellish strongholds fierce fighting broke out as remnants of the Xaghash (lesser Darklords) and the Nadziranim (evil practitioners of Right-handed magic who once aided individual Darklord masters) fought for control. It is widely believed that by the time the Elder Magi and the Herbwardens reach the walls of these strongholds the occupants will have long since brought about their own extinction.

Elsewhere, throughout northern Magnamund, peace reigns victorious and the peoples of the Free Kingdoms rejoice in the knowledge that the age of the Darklords has finally come to an end. Readily men have exchanged their swords for hoes and their shields for ploughs, and now the only marching they do is along the ruts of their freshly furrowed fields. Few are the watchful eyes that scan the distant horizon in fear of what may appear, although there are still those who maintain their vigilance, for the agents of Naar come in many guises and there are those who wait quietly in the shadows for the chance to do his evil bidding.

Only six months ago the evil Cener Druids of Ruel attempted to enact Naar's revenge. Secretly, in the laboratories of their foul stronghold of Mogaruith, they had laboured to create a virulent plague virus capable of killing every living creature upon Magnamund, save their own kind. Word of their terrible plan reached Lord Rimoah who immediately urged the rulers of the Freelands to raise armies and invade Ruel. Hurriedly they complied, but the invasion ended in disaster. Seven thousand fighting men entered Ruel intent on storming the fortress of Mogaruith and razing it to the ground. Seven thousand marched into the dark realm; only seventy emerged alive. The Ceners were within days of perfecting their ultimate weapon when you took up the challenge and ventured alone into Mogaruith. Despite overwhelming odds you thwarted their evil plan by destroying the virus and the means by which it was created.

After emerging from Ruel triumphant, your quest fulfilled, you returned home to Sommerlund and the Kai monastery where you resumed your duties as Grand Master. Three months later, on the day that saw the first fall of winter snow, you were visited by Lord Rimoah. Once again he found himself the reluctant bearer of ill news. Your friend Guildmaster Banedon, whilst helping with the reclamation of wastelands close to the Maakengorge, had been abducted by a war-band of Giaks under the command of Nadziranim sorcerers. A rescue was attempted, but ruthlessly the Nadziranim obliterated those who tried to follow their escape into the Darklands.

"The Nadziranim have grown bold of late," said Lord Rimoah, his words tinged with fear and bitterness. "They have a new-found power and are keen to exercise it. It would have taken considerable skill and energy to ensnare one as gifted as Banedon."

"But why Banedon?" you asked, trying at once to comprehend and come to terms with the loss of your trusted friend.

"I fear that the Nadziranim seek to extract from him the secrets of Left-handed magic, so that they may be able to marry it to their own foul sorcery. Such an outcome would give them extraordinary power. It could herald the re-birth of the Darklands."

At once you recalled how such an attempt to unite the two paths of magic had resulted in catastrophe for Sommerlund. Vonotar the Traitor, a magician from the same guild as Banedon, had betrayed his homeland in exchange for the promise of Nadziranim power. It was his act of treachery that brought about the invasion of Sommerlund and the destruction of the First Order of the Kai.

"What can be done?" you asked of Rimoah, fearful that it may already be too late to save your friend.

"Banedon is still alive, of that I'm sure. The Nadziranim have taken him to the old Darklord city-fortress of Kaag. His life is in deadly danger but they will not kill him until they have succeeded in extracting the knowledge they crave. We can only pray that he is strong enough to resist them until..." Lord Rimoah held you with his eyes, words no longer necessary. It was clear that all hope for Banedon's survival depended upon his swift rescue from Kaag, and there was only one who could effect such a perilous quest with any hope of success.

"So be it," you said, resolutely, "I accept the mission. I alone will go to Kaag and secure his release ... or die valiantly in the attempt."

THE GAME RULES

You keep a record of your adventure on the *Action Chart* that you will find in the front of this book. For ease of use, and for further adventuring, it is recommended that you photocopy these pages.

For more than five years, ever since the demise of the Darklords of Helgedad, you have devoted yourself to developing further your fighting prowess—COMBAT SKILL—and physical stamina—ENDURANCE. Before you begin this Grand Master adventure you need to measure how effective your training has been. To do this, take a pencil and, with your eyes closed, point with the blunt end of it on to the *Random Number Table* on the last page of this book. If you pick a *0* it counts as zero.

The first number that you pick from the *Random Number Table* in this way represents your COMBAT SKILL. Add 25 to the number you picked and write the total in the COMBAT SKILL section of your *Action Chart* (ie, if your pencil fell on the number 6 in the *Random Number Table* you would write in a COMBAT SKILL of 31). When you fight, your COMBAT SKILL will be pitted against that of your enemy. A high score in this section is therefore very desirable.

The second number that you pick from the *Random Number Table* represents your powers of ENDURANCE. Add 30 to this number and write the total in the ENDURANCE section of your *Action Chart* (ie, if your pencil fell on the number 7 on the *Random Number Table* you would have 37 ENDURANCE points).

If you are wounded in combat you will lose ENDURANCE points. If at any time your ENDURANCE points fall to zero, you are dead and the adventure is over. Lost ENDURANCE points can be regained during the course of the adventure, but your number of ENDURANCE points can not rise above the number you have when you start an adventure.

If you have successfully completed any of the previous adventures in the *Lone Wolf* series (Books 1–13), you can carry your current scores of COMBAT SKILL and EN-DURANCE points over to Book 14. These scores may include Weaponmastery, Curing, and Psi-surge bonuses obtained upon completion of *Lone Wolf Kai* (Books 1–5) or *Magnakai* (Books 6–12) adventures. Only if you have completed these previous adventures will you benefit from the appropriate bonuses in the course of the Grand Master series. You may also carry over any Weapons and Backpack Items you had in your possession at the end of your last adventure, and these should be entered on your new Grand Master *Action Chart* (you are still limited to two Weapons, but you may now carry up to ten Backpack Items).

However, only the following Special Items may be carried over from the *Lone Wolf Kai* (1–5) and *Magnakai* (6–12) series to the *Lone Wolf* Grand Master series (13–onwards):

CRYSTAL STAR PENDANT	JEWELLED MACE
SOMMERSWERD	SILVER BOW OF DUADON
SILVER HELM	HELSHEZAG
DAGGER OF VASHNA	KAGONITE CHAINMAIL

8

KAI AND MAGNAKAI DISCIPLINES

During your distinguished rise to the rank of Kai Grand Master, you have become proficient in all of the basic Kai and Magnakai Disciplines. These Disciplines have provided you with a formidable arsenal of natural abilities which have served you well in the fight against the agents and champions of Naar, King of the Darkness. A brief summary of your skills is given below.

Weaponmastery
Proficiency with all close combat and missile weapons. Master of unarmed combat; no COMBAT SKILL loss when fighting bare-handed.

Animal Control
Communication with most animals; limited control over hostile creatures. Can use woodland animals as guides and can block a non-sentient creature's sense of taste and smell.

Curing
Steady restoration of lost ENDURANCE points (to self and others) as a result of combat wounds. Neutralization of poisons, venoms and toxins. Repair of serious battle wounds.

Invisibility
Mask body heat and scent; hide effectively; mask sounds during movement; minor alterations of physical appearance.

Huntmastery
Effective hunting of food in the wild; increased agility; intensified vision, hearing, smell and night vision.

Pathsmanship

Read languages, decipher symbols, read footprints and tracks. Intuitive knowledge of compass points; detection of enemy ambush up to 500 yards; ability to cross terrain without leaving tracks; converse with sentient creatures; mask self from psychic spells of detection.

Psi-surge

Attack enemies using the powers of the mind; set up disruptive vibrations in objects; confuse enemies.

Psi-screen

Defence against hypnosis, supernatural illusions, charms, hostile telepathy and evil spirits. Ability to divert and re-channel hostile psychic energy.

Nexus

Move small items by projection of mind power; withstand extremes of temperature; extinguish fire by force of will; limited immunity to flames, toxic gases, corrosive liquids.

Divination

Sense imminent danger; detect invisible or hidden enemy; telepathic communication; recognize magic-using and/or magical creatures; detect psychic residues; limited ability to leave body and spirit-walk.

GRAND MASTER DISCIPLINES

Now, through the pursuit of new skills and the further development of your innate Kai abilities, you have set out upon a path of discovery that no other Kai Grand Master has ever attempted with success. Your determination to become the first Kai Supreme Master, by acquiring total proficiency in all twelve of the Grand Master Disciplines, is an awe-inspiring challenge. You will be venturing into the unknown, pushing back the boundaries of human limitation in the pursuit of greatness and the cause of Good. May the blessings of the gods Kai and Ishir go with you as you begin your brave and noble quest.

In the years following the demise of the Darklords you have reached the rank of Kai Grand Defender, which means that you have mastered *four* of the Grand Master Disciplines listed below. It is up to you to choose which four Disciplines these are. As all of the Grand Master Disciplines will be of use to you at some point during your adventure, pick your four skills with care. The correct use of a Grand Master Discipline at the right time could save your life.

When you have chosen your four Disciplines, enter them in the Grand Master Disciplines section of your *Action Chart*.

Grand Weaponmastery

This Discipline enables a Grand Master to become supremely efficient in the use of all weapons. When you enter combat with one of your Grand Master weapons, you add 5 points to your COMBAT SKILL. The rank of Kai Grand Defender, with which you begin the Grand Master series, means you are skilled in *two* of the weapons listed overleaf.

Animal Mastery

Grand Masters have considerable control over hostile, non-sentient creatures. Also, they have the ability to converse with birds and fishes, and use them as guides.

Deliverance (*Advanced Curing*)

Grand Masters are able to use their healing power to repair serious battle wounds. If, whilst in combat, their ENDURANCE points are reduced to 8 points or less, they can draw upon their mastery to restore 20 ENDURANCE points. This ability can only be used once every 20 days.

SPEAR

DAGGER

MACE

SHORT SWORD

WARHAMMER

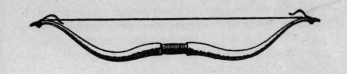

BOW

QUARTERSTAFF

BROADSWORD

AXE

SWORD

Assimilance (*Advanced Invisibility*)

Grand Masters are able to effect striking changes to their physical appearance, and maintain these changes over a period of a few days. They have also mastered advanced camouflage techniques that make them virtually undetectable in an open landscape.

Grand Huntmastery

Grand Masters are able to see in total darkness, and have greatly heightened senses of touch and taste.

Grand Pathsmanship

Grand Masters are able to resist entrapment by hostile plants, and have a super-awareness of ambush, or the threat of ambush, in woods and dense forests.

Kai-surge

When using their psychic ability to attack an enemy, Grand Masters may add 8 points to their COMBAT SKILL. For every round in which Kai-surge is used, Grand Masters need only deduct 1 ENDURANCE point. When using the weaker psychic attack—Mindblast—they may add 4 points without loss of ENDURANCE points. (Kai-surge, Psi-surge, and Mindblast cannot be used simultaneously.)

Grand Masters cannot use Kai-surge if their ENDURANCE score falls to 6 points or below.

Kai-screen

In psychic combat, Grand Masters are able to construct mind fortresses capable of protecting themselves and others. The strength and capacity of these fortresses increases as a Grand Master advances in rank.

Grand Nexus

Grand Masters are able to withstand contact with harmful elements, such as flames and acids, for upwards of an hour in duration. This ability increases as a Grand Master advances in rank.

Telegnosis (*Advanced Divination*)
This Discipline enables a Grand Master to spirit-walk for far greater lengths of time, and with far fewer ill effects. Duration, and the protection of his inanimate body, increases as a Grand Master advances in rank.

Magi-Magic
Under the tutelage of Lord Rimoah, you have been able to master the rudimentary skills of battle magic, as taught to the Vakeros—the native warriors of Dessi. As you advance in rank, so will your knowledge and mastery of Old Kingdom magic increase.

Kai-alchemy
Under the tutelage of Guildmaster Banedon, you have mastered the elementary spells of Left-handed magic, as practised by the Brotherhood of the Crystal Star. As you advance in rank, so will your knowledge and mastery of Left-handed magic increase, enabling you to craft new Kai weapons and artifacts.

If you successfully complete the mission as set in Book 14 of the *Lone Wolf* Grand Master series, you may add a further Grand Master Discipline of your choice to your *Action Chart* in Book 15.

For every Grand Master Discipline you possess, in excess of the original four Disciplines you begin with, you may add 1 point to your basic COMBAT SKILL score and 2 points to your basic ENDURANCE points score. These bonus points, together with your extra Grand Master Discipline(s), your original four Grand Master Disciplines, and any Special Items that you have found and been able to keep during your adventures, may then be carried over and used in the next Grand Master adventure, which is called *The Darke Crusade*.

EQUIPMENT

Before you leave the monastery and journey westwards to Kaag, you take with you a map of the Darklands (see inside front cover of this book) and a pouch of gold. To find out how much gold is in the pouch, pick a number from the *Random Number Table* and add 20 to the number you have picked. The total equals the number of Gold Crowns inside the pouch, and you should now enter this number in the *"Gold Crowns"* section of your *Action Chart*.

If you have successfully completed any of the previous *Lone Wolf* adventures (Books 1–13), you may add this sum to the total sum of Crowns you already possess. Fifty Crowns is the maximum you can carry, but additional Crowns can be left in safe-keeping at your monastery.

You can take five items from the list below, again adding to these, if necessary, any you may already possess from previous adventures. (Remember, you are still limited to two Weapons, but you may now carry a maximum of ten Backpack Items).

SWORD (Weapons)
BOW (Weapons)
QUIVER (Special Items) This contains six arrows; record them on your Weapons List.

AXE (Weapons)

4 MEALS (Meals) Each Meal takes up one space in your
   Backpack.

ROPE (Backpack Item)

POTION OF LAUMSPUR (Backpack Item) This potion restores 4
   ENDURANCE points to your total when swallowed after
   combat. There is enough for only one dose.

SPEAR (Weapons)
DAGGER (Weapons)

List the five items that you choose on your *Action Chart*,
under the appropriate headings, and make a note of any
effect they may have on your ENDURANCE points or COMBAT
SKILL.

How to use your equipment

Weapons

The maximum number of weapons that you can carry is *two*. Weapons aid you in combat. If you have the Grand Master Discipline of Grand Weaponmastery and a correct weapon, it adds 5 points to your COMBAT SKILL. If you find a weapon during your adventure, you may pick it up and use it.

Bows and Arrows

During your adventure there will be opportunities to use a bow and arrow. If you equip yourself with this weapon, and you possess at least one arrow, you may use it when the text of a particular section allows you to do so. The bow is a useful weapon, for it enables you to hit an enemy at a distance. However, a bow cannot be used in hand-to-hand combat, therefore it is strongly recommended that you also equip yourself with a close combat weapon, such as a sword or an axe.

In order to use a bow you must possess a quiver and at least one arrow. Each time the bow is used, erase an arrow from your *Action Chart*. A bow cannot, of course, be used if you exhaust your supply of arrows, but the opportunity may arise during your adventure for you to replenish your stock of arrows.

If you have the Discipline of Grand Weaponmastery with a bow, you may add 3 points to any number that you pick from the *Random Number Table*, when using the bow.

Backpack Items

These must be stored in your Backpack. Because space is limited, you may keep a maximum of ten articles, including Meals, in your Backpack at any one time. You may carry only one Backpack at a time. During your travels you will discover various useful items which you may decide to keep.

You may exchange or discard them at any point when you are not involved in combat.

Any item that may be of use, and which can be picked up on your adventure and entered on your *Action Chart* is given either initial capitals (eg Gold Dagger, Magic Pendant), or is clearly labelled as a Backpack Item. Unless you are told that it is a Special Item, carry it in your Backpack.

Special Items
Special Items are not carried in the Backpack. When you discover a Special Item, you will be told how or where to carry it. The maximum number of Special Items that can be carried on any adventure is twelve.

Food
Food is carried in your Backpack. Each Meal counts as one item. You will need to eat regularly during your adventure. If you do not have any food when you are instructed to eat a Meal, you will lose 3 ENDURANCE points. However, if you have chosen the Discipline of Grand Huntmastery, you will not need to tick off a Meal when instructed to eat.

Potion of Laumspur
This is a healing potion that can restore 4 ENDURANCE points to your total when swallowed after combat. There is enough for one dose only. If you discover any other potion during the adventure, you will be informed of its effect. All potions are Backpack Items.

RULES FOR COMBAT

There will be occasions during your adventure when you have to fight an enemy. The enemy's COMBAT SKILL and ENDURANCE points are given in the text. Lone Wolf's aim in

19

the combat is to kill the enemy by reducing his ENDURANCE points to zero while losing as few ENDURANCE points as possible himself.

At the start of a combat, enter Lone Wolf's and the enemy's ENDURANCE points in the appropriate boxes on the "Combat Record" section of your Action Chart.

The sequence for combat is as follows:

1. Add any extra points gained through your Grand Master Disciplines and Special Items to your current COMBAT SKILL total.

2. Subtract the COMBAT SKILL of your enemy from this total. The result is your Combat Ratio. Enter it on the Action Chart.

Example

Lone Wolf (COMBAT SKILL 32) is attacked by a pack of Doomwolves (COMBAT SKILL 30). He is taken by surprise and is not given the opportunity of evading their attack. Lone Wolf has the Grand Master Discipline of Kai-surge to which the Doomwolves are not immune, so Lone Wolf adds 8 points to his COMBAT SKILL, giving him a total COMBAT SKILL of 40.

He subtracts the Doomwolf pack's COMBAT SKILL from his own, giving a Combat Ratio of $+10$. $(40-30 = +10)$. $+10$ is noted on the Action Chart as the Combat Ratio.

3. When you have your Combat Ratio, pick a number from the Random Number Table.

4. Turn to the COMBAT RESULTS TABLE at the back of this book. Along the top of the chart are shown the Combat

Ratio numbers. Find the number that is the same as your *Combat Ratio* and cross-reference it with the random number that you have picked. (The random numbers appear on the side of the chart.) You now have the number of ENDURANCE points lost by both Lone Wolf and his enemy in this round of combat. (*E* represents points lost by the enemy; *LW* represents points lost by Lone Wolf.)

Example
The *Combat Ratio* between Lone Wolf and The Doom-wolf Pack has been established as +10. If the number taken from the *Random Number Table* is a 2, then the result of the first round of combat is:

Lone Wolf loses 3 ENDURANCE points (plus an additional 1 point for using Kai-surge).
Doomwolf Pack loses 9 ENDURANCE points.

5. On the *Action Chart*, mark the changes in ENDURANCE points to the participants in the combat.

6. Unless otherwise instructed, or unless you have an option to evade, the next round of combat now starts.

7. Repeat the sequence from Stage 3.

This process of combat continues until ENDURANCE points of either the enemy or Lone Wolf are reduced to zero, at which point the one with the zero score is declared dead. If Lone Wolf is dead, the adventure is over. If the enemy is dead, Lone Wolf proceeds but with his ENDURANCE points reduced.

A summary of Combat Rules also appears at the back of the book.

Evasion of combat
During your adventure you may be given the chance to

evade combat. If you have already engaged in a round of combat and decide to evade, calculate the combat for that round in the usual manner. All points lost by the enemy as a result of that round are ignored, and you make your escape. Only Lone Wolf may lose ENDURANCE points during that round (but then that is the risk of running away!). You may evade only if the text of the particular section allows you to do so.

GRAND MASTER'S WISDOM

Your mission to enter old Darklord city-fortress of Kaag and rescue Guildmaster Banedon will be fraught with deadly dangers. Be wary and on your guard at all times, for the inhabitants of Kaag are still a formidable enemy despite the demise of their Darklord masters.

Some of the things that you will find during your mission will be of use to you in this and future *Lone Wolf* books, while others may be red herrings of no real value at all, so try to be selective in what you decide to keep.

Choose your four Grand Master Disciplines with care, for a wise choice will enable any player to complete the quest, no matter how weak their initial COMBAT SKILL and ENDURANCE scores may be. Successful completion of previous *Lone Wolf* adventures, although an advantage, is not essential for the completion of this *Grand Master* adventure.

The survival of your countryman and close friend Banedon depends on the success of your mission. May the light of Kai and Ishir be your guide as you venture into the grim darkness of Kaag.

For Sommerlund and the Kai!

IMPROVED GRAND MASTER DISCIPLINES

As you rise through the higher levels of Kai Grand Mastery, you will find that your Disciplines will steadily improve. For example, if you possess the Discipline of Grand Nexus when you reach the Grand Master rank of Grand Thane, you will be able to pass freely through Shadow Gates and explore the nether realms of Aon and the Daziarn Plane.

If you are a Grand Master who has reached the rank of Kai Grand Guardian, you will now benefit from improvements to the following Grand Master Disciplines:

Animal Mastery
Kai Grand Guardians with this Discipline are able to summon a limited number of forest animals to their location. The creatures so summoned will become loyal and willing allies, eager to do the Kai Grand Guardian's bidding. This ability can only be used in an outdoor setting.

Assimilance
Kai Grand Guardians who possess this skill are able to create a cloud of fog-like vapour within 15 yards of their location. This fog will obscure both normal and infra-vision. The duration of the fog increases as a Grand Master rises in rank.

Grand Huntmastery
Kai Grand Guardians with this skill enjoy increased mobility when travelling across all types of terrain, whether on foot or on horseback. This improved ability is very useful when used to outdistance a pursuing enemy.

Kai-surge

Kai Grand Guardians who possess mastery of this Discipline are able to attack up to three enemies in psychic combat simultaneously.

Kai-screen

Kai Grand Guardians who possess this Discipline are able to exercise a defensive psychic skill known as Mind-blend. This cloaking ability enables them to both protect and hide their minds from being detected by a hostile psychic probe.

Magi-Magic

Grand Masters who have reached the rank of Kai Grand Guardian are able to use the following battle-spells of the Elder Magi:

Splinter—This causes breakable items such as bottles, jugs, mirrors, windows, etc, to shatter to pieces. The range of this spell increases as a Grand Master rises in rank.

Flameshaft—This causes the tip of any arrow, or arrow-like missile, to burn fiercely with a magical flame which cannot readily be extinguished by normal means.

The nature of these additional improvements and how they affect your Grand Master Disciplines will be noted in the "Improved Grand Master Disciplines" section of future *Lone Wolf* books.

LEVELS OF KAI GRAND MASTERSHIP

The following table is a guide to the rank and titles you can achieve at each stage of your journey along the road of Kai Grand Mastership. As you complete each adventure successfully in the *Lone Wolf Grand Master* series, you will gain an additional Grand Master Discipline and progress towards the pinnacle of Kai perfection—to become a Kai Supreme Master.

No. of Grand Master Disciplines acquired	Grand Master Rank
1	Kai Grand Master Senior
2	Kai Grand Master Superior
3	Kai Grand Sentinel
4	Kai Grand Defender—*You begin the Lone Wolf Grand Master adventures at this level of Mastery*
5	Kai Grand Guardian
6	Sun Knight
7	Sun Lord
8	Sun Thane
9	Grand Thane
10	Grand Crown
11	Sun Prince
12	Kai Supreme Master

1

Preparations for the quest take no more than a day to complete. The following morning, shortly before dawn, you and Lord Rimoah leave the Kai monastery by a secret route which takes you to a clearing deep in the heart of the Fryelund forest. There awaits the means by which you will travel swiftly to Kaag.

Your journey to the Darklands will be made aboard Guildmaster Banedon's airship—the *Skyrider*. This magical craft has borne you on many quests to distant lands, yet never before without your friend and companion at its helm. Now, in his absence, the stewardship of the *Skyrider* has passed to its Bo'sun—Nolrim of Bor.

"Welcome aboard, Grand Master," says Nolrim, proud to be serving under your command. You clasp his strong hand in friendship and compliment him and the crew for the pristine condition of their craft. There is no doubting that he and his company of dwarves are sorely grieved by the absence of their Captain, yet they have not allowed their anguish to give way to hopelessness or despair. These sturdy warriors are renowned for their formidable fighting spirit and you know they willingly risk their lives to help you rescue Banedon from the minions of darkness.

1

Soon the frost-laden fir trees are receding beneath the *Sky-rider's* bow as Nolrim steers a westward course towards the grey, snow-capped peaks of the Durncrag mountains. You spend the flight inside the Captain's cabin, where you and Lord Rimoah discuss your dangerous mission. The plan is to traverse the Durncrag Range and enter the Darklands under cover of a dust storm which is currently sweeping southwards towards Kaag. A landing will be made ten miles to the north-east of the city-fortress, beyond a ridge of hills that will keep the *Skyrider* hidden from the eyes of Kaag's watchful look-outs. From there you are to make your way to the fortress on foot, enter as best you can, locate and rescue Banedon, then return with him to the *Skyrider* which will carry you back to the safety of Sommerlund. You will have 48 hours in which to complete your mission. If, after the two days have elapsed, you have not returned, Rimoah will be forced to assume that you and the Guildmaster have perished. The dust storm will not last for more than two days, after which time there is a grave danger that the *Skyrider* will be spotted and attacked by the Kraan and Zlanbeasts which are known to patrol the skies around Kaag.

In a little under two hours you reach your destination where the weather conditions are atrocious. A fierce, dust-choked wind buffets the craft mercilessly during the final descent and visibility is no more than a dozen yards at best. Yet, despite these terrible conditions, Nolrim brings the *Skyrider* in for a faultless landing behind the ridge. The moment the keel beds into the soft ground, the crew leap into action with ropes and chains. Nolrim soon enters the cabin to inform you that the craft is secure and, with trepidation, you get ready to set off for Kaag.

"Godspeed, Lone Wolf," says Rimoah, with a smile of encouragement. "I shall pray to Kai and Ishir for your safety and success. May their light guide you on your journey into darkness."

You acknowledge his blessing gratefully before bidding him, and Nolrim, farewell. Then, without looking back, you pull your warm cloak tight about you and set off into the storm.

Turn to **267**.

2

The sound of arrows whistling towards your back provides all the incentive you need to keep running. You bound up the steps and, as the deadly barbed shafts fly past only inches from your back and legs, you run headlong into the tunnel.

The dingy passage beyond descends by slope and stair to a rectangular hall which is lined with ancient stone statues, their features made unrecognizable by age. Tar-soaked torches fixed to the two longest walls illuminate this musty chamber with a flickering amber light, and the air is heavy with their oily stench. In the distance you see an archway and the passage continuing away into darkness.

If you wish to stop here for a few minutes and try to revive Banedon, turn to **25**.
If you decide to press on without stopping here, turn to **151**.

3

On the third tap the lock emits a distinct *click* and, slowly, the great door swings open to reveal a dark, smoky tunnel. Warily you pass through the door and enter this unwelcoming passage.

Turn to **171**.

4

You run into a passageway and follow it towards a distant intersection, but as you near the end of this narrow thoroughfare, a figure clad in red robes, accompanied by three Giaks, suddenly appears from the right and blocks your path. At once you recognize the robed creature: it is a Vordak, an undead spawn of the Darklords. The instant it sees you it attempts to cut you down with a bolt of psychic energy, but your innate Magnakai defences negate this attack. Shocked by your immunity to its power, the Vordak scans your mind and instantly discovers your true identity. With a shriek of abject horror the creature turns and flees, leaving its Giak escort stunned and bewildered by its behaviour. Then, too, their nerve breaks and they scurry after their lieutenant as fast as their bowed legs will carry them.

Anxious to prevent them from escaping and raising the alarm, you chase them towards a junction at the end of the street. When they reach the junction they split up; the Vordak turns to the left, while the three Giaks head off to the right.

If you wish to pursue the Vordak, turn to **102**.
If you choose to pursue the Giaks, turn to **162**.

5

Defiantly you raise your right hand and point your finger at the Helghast's chest. The creature sneers, revealing two sharp fangs which protrude from its lower jaw. It emits a hideous cackle, full of hatred and contempt, and its eyes blaze like two hot coals as it confidently quickens its gait. You utter the words of power that you learned from your mentor, Guildmaster Banedon, and at once your whole hand is sleeved with a crackling blue-white fire. A jolt runs the length of your arm and a pulse of energy, shaped like a small meteor, arcs from your index finger towards the approaching Helghast. The bolt rips through its chest and, with a wail of abject terror, the creature is lifted into the air and sent tumbling backwards into the flame-filled moat.

Open-mouthed, the two Drakkarim stumble to a halt and stare down into the all-consuming fire. Nervously they glance at each other, fearful of suffering a similar fate, but years of fierce battle discipline soon override their anxiety and, like two automatons, they raise their swords and continue to advance towards you.

Drakkarim veterans:
COMBAT SKILL 30   ENDURANCE 35

If you win this combat, turn to **293**.

6

You raise the sun-sword and the onrushing bolt of energy is drawn to its blade where it collides with a brilliant flash, showering you with sparks which rapidly dissolve. Power surges through the hilt of your divine sword and flows along your arm, renewing your flagging strength: increase your ENDURANCE points score by 3.

Revitalized by this energy, you bite back your fear and focus on the advancing swarm. Suddenly your psychic senses tingle. These are no ordinary insects; in fact these are not insects at all. Your sixth sense detects that they are merely a clever illusion created to deceive you. Confident in this knowledge, you stand your ground and allow the tide of creepy-crawlies to wash over your feet. Within a matter of seconds the insect horde fades and vanishes, dispelled by your disbelief in their existence.

Turn to **243**.

7

On the seventh tap, there is a loud *click* and the heavy steel door creaks slowly open. Ahead you see a ramp which slopes down to a junction where a passage crosses from left to right. You descend the slope, taking care not to graze Banedon's back against the low ceiling, and when you reach the junction you ask your friend in which direction you should go. Unfortunately your question goes unanswered; Banedon has lapsed once more into unconsciousness.

You stand at the junction and use your Kai senses in an attempt to choose the safest route, but you detect nothing that can help or influence your decision. Both routes seem equally unwelcoming and perilous.

If you decide to turn left, turn to **235**.
If you choose to go right, turn to **72**.

8

Aided by your youthful strength and Kai skills, you catch hold of the archway and pull yourself to safety. After pausing just long enough to catch your breath, you look into the dust-filled room and reflect upon how you were nearly buried alive. With a shake of your head you dismiss these morbid thoughts and set off along the tunnel.

Turn to **71**.

9

You pull yourself over the parapet, only to be confronted immediately by a Drakkar guard. Unbeknown to you he has been sitting on the tower roof, quietly watching the spectacle of the feeding Kraan.

He grabs you by the throat and attempts to throw you off the tower. You counter this clumsy attack easily by turning his hand aside and grabbing hold of his battle tunic. A swift twist of your body sends him sailing over your shoulder to land, head first, in the street below.

The guard, his neck broken, is no longer a threat to anyone, so you turn your attention to the five Kraan which are feeding on the roof. Gingerly you approach them, hoping not to startle them into flight, but the commotion, and your presence, has made them very uneasy.

If you possess the Discipline of Animal Mastery, turn to **78**.
If you do not possess this skill, turn to **118**.

10

You search for a weak spot on the creature's shell but you cannot readily discern one. The tip of your arrow is made of best Sommlending steel but, even so, you fear it may not be sufficient to penetrate the creature's chest.

If you possess Kai-alchemy, and have reached the rank of Kai Grand Guardian, turn to **195**.
If you do not possess this skill, or have not yet reached this Kai rank, turn to **63**.

11

You raise your weapon to defend yourself from the creature's attack but, as you stare into its hellish eyes, you suddenly realize that this supernatural horror is immune to the effects of man-made weaponry.

If you possess the Dagger of Vashna, a Jewelled Mace, or the Sword of Helshezag, turn to **285**.
If you do not possess one of these Special Items, turn to **181**.

12

Before you can find something with which to start a fire, the octopoid moves away from the pool and forces you back against the wall of rubble. You contemplate escaping through the narrow gap by which you entered the chamber but it is already too late; the creature's tentacles are almost upon you.

Resigned to your fate, you unsheathe your weapon and prepare to face this hideous being in mortal combat.

Korozon: COMBAT SKILL 52   ENDURANCE 45

This creature is immune to all forms of psychic attack.

If you win the combat, turn to **68**.

13

The Liganim watch you return to Banedon, then they turn and flee through the archway. Less than a minute later they return with a troop of armoured Drakkarim and Giak soldiers. Like a horde of screaming fanatics, they come rushing down the staircase and spread out to surround you and your companion. You draw your weapon and fight bravely, dispatching more than fifty of the enemy, but they receive a constant stream of reinforcements and, when finally your strength fails you, you are overwhelmed by these merciless denizens of Kaag.

Tragically, your life and your quest end here.

14

Your desperate attempts to reach the saddle are dashed when the Kraan rears up in the air and rakes you with its claws. You lose your grip and fall screaming to the concourse below.

You hit the ground and instantly lose consciousness. Tragically, although you survive the fall, you never reawaken. Your body is discovered by a Giak patrol who kill you out of hand, thinking you to be an enemy spy in disguise.

Your life and your quest end here before the citadel of Kaag.

15

The arrow strikes the creature in the centre of its forehead but causes it no injury. With a dull *crack* the tip snaps off and the shaft ricochets harmlessly away. There is no time now for a second shot so you hurriedly shoulder your bow and draw a hand weapon. Sensing victory within its grasp, the creature emits a gurgling shriek and comes bounding forwards. You get ready to meet its advance; however, when it is only ten feet away, it suddenly opens its mouth wide and spews forth a stream of white-hot liquid fire.

If you possess the Discipline of Grand Nexus, turn to **288**.
If you do not possess this Grand Master Discipline, turn to **248**.

16

The sensation of danger is steadily building. Fearful that the denizens of this domain may burst into the hall and thwart your rescue attempt at any moment, you cast the Brotherhood spell *"Detect Evil"* in the hope of locating exactly where the danger lies.

Unfortunately, the spell merely serves to increase the sensitivity of your Kai senses. The sensation of impending danger becomes like a heavy cloud that is suffocating you. Gasping for breath, you are forced to break off the spell for fear of losing consciousness: deduct 1 ENDURANCE point.

If you possess Telegnosis, and wish to use it, turn to **237**.
If you do not possess this Discipline, or choose not to use it, turn to **127**.

17

The door opens on your seventeenth knock, revealing a small armoury beyond. Most of the weapons stored here are of inferior quality, but you do notice several which may be of use to you during your quest:

4 Arrows
1 Quiver
Sword
Dagger
Broadsword

If you wish to keep any of the above, remember to adjust your *Action Chart* accordingly.

On the far side of this armoury you discover a spiral staircase.

If you wish to ascend the stairs, turn to **266**.
If you choose to descend the stairs, turn to **132**.

18

A wave of negative psychic energy crashes against your mind, forcing you to erect a defensive wall to prevent it from damaging your nervous system. You muster your psychic reserves in preparation yet, as the complex process is taking place, you suddenly realize that you are playing into your unseen enemy's hands.

You sense that your attacker feeds off psychic defences; to erect a mind-wall would merely provide power for the creature to gorge itself upon. Mindful of this fact you consciously deplete your mind-wall, draining the energy away, channelling it to boost your Kai senses instead.

Your strategy works; the creature breaks off its psychic attack (increase your current ENDURANCE by 4 points). The creature then prepares to attack you face to face.

Turn to **196**.

19—*Illustration I (overleaf)*

You race across the mound of jagged rubble, barely slowing your stride as you surmount this obstacle easily. The pursuing Death Knights, handicapped by their weighty armour and lack of special skills, can only watch in astonishment as you disappear from view.

The street continues beyond the mound, heading due south towards the great citadel, the shadow of this edifice looming ever larger. Soon the street opens out to a wide concourse which encircles the citadel and offers access to its great northern door. The entire door is made of black iron and streaked with rust. Turrets jut from either side, on top of which you see giant cannon-like weapons, similar to those once employed by the Darklords aboard their ironclad fleets.

From the cover of a ruined house, you watch the traffic of Giaks and Drakkarim, all clad in orange uniforms bearing the mark of a bloodied scythe. The more you stare at the citadel, the more you are sure that this is where Banedon is being held prisoner. However, entry into the citadel itself looks to be impossible, until, that is, an opportunity unexpectedly presents itself.

Turn to **107**.

20

Your spell causes the crystal to vibrate, but you are too weak to muster the power needed to shatter or dislodge it. The curtain of light imprisoning Banedon remains intact and you are forced to abandon the spell and try some other way of freeing him.

If you possess a Bow and wish to use it, turn to **211**.
If you possess Kai-alchemy, and have reached the rank of Kai Grand Guardian, turn to **60**.
If you do not have a Bow, do not possess Kai-alchemy, or have yet to reach the required Kai rank, turn instead to **292**.

I. Giaks and Drakkarim pass the citadel, all clad in orange uniforms bearing the mark of a bloodied scythe.

21

You descend ten levels and follow a tunnel which eventually ends at a sealed door, carved from a solid slab of coal-black steel. Engraved into its surface are several runes and glyphs of power which you immediately recognize to be magical. They have been placed here as a warning to anyone foolish enough to attempt a forced entry that such an attempt is likely to result in their death.

Intrigued by the warning, you examine the runes more closely. As you are doing so, you suddenly hear a sound in the tunnel and turn to see two figures approaching. Hurriedly you retreat into the shadows, masking yourself with your camouflage disciplines to prevent your detection, as the two figures draw closer to the door.

Turn to **234**.

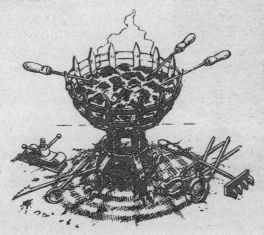

22

The challenge catches you off-guard and your mind races for an answer that you hope will sound convincing.

"I've been sent here by my master to deliver an unholy relic," you say, patting your canvas haversack.

The two guards stare at the satchel then look at each other and converse in a language you do not recognize.

Pick a number from the *Random Number Table*. If you possess Kai-alchemy or Assimilance, add 2 to the number you have picked.

If total score is now 5 or less, turn to **206**.
If it is 6 or more, turn to **85**.

23

You push Banedon aside and dive to avoid the falling trap but, even though you act speedily, your legs are ensnared by the net and you are brought crashing to your knees.

"Finish them both!" snarls a voice, and a dozen trident-wielding Drakkarim leap from the shadows, eager to enact their master's command.

Turn to **155**.

24

Your invisible shield fails to protect you fully against all of the speeding crossbow bolts. One penetrates its weakened bottom edge, bursting through with a splash of yellow sparks to gouge your thigh: lose 2 ENDURANCE points.

Biting back the pain, you hurry towards the Death Knights, hoping to break through their line before they have a chance to reload and fire again. The sight of you surviving such a rain of missiles leaves many of their number staring open-mouthed with shock. You dodge through their line with ease, and by the time they realize that you have evaded them, and start to give chase, you have passed the junction and begun to run along the street opposite.

Turn to **230**.

You lower Banedon to the floor and make him as comfortable as you can by propping him in a sitting position with his back against one of the statues. Then, despite your own fatigue, you use your innate healing skills in an attempt to revive him to consciousness. His pulse is weak and his skin is cold to the touch, and you can tell by his poor physical condition that he has been starved and beaten during his imprisonment here in Kaag. Placing your hands upon his brow, you feel some of your body warmth draining away as you concentrate on transmitting your healing powers to your injured friend. Slowly he responds, and although he is still too weak to speak, he manages to open his eyes and communicate with you telepathically.

"I know this chamber ..." he says, *"... I have been here before. Look there, at the statue opposite. You'll find a lever concealed at its side. It opens a hidden door."*

Guided by Banedon's messages you discover that there is indeed a lever as he described. You pull it and a panel in the stone wall glides open to reveal a secret alcove and flight of steps leading downwards. Noises in the tunnel warn you that Drakkarim are approaching and so, without hesitation, you shoulder your friend once more and hurry into the alcove to avoid them.

Turn to **188**.

26

Fear rapidly turns to panic as the loathsome tide of insects comes crawling and scuttling towards your legs. You cast your eyes left and right, seeking escape, but before you can turn and run, you become the target of a new attack. From out of the hovering shadow there comes a crackling bolt of energy. Quickly it gathers speed as it hurtles directly towards your head.

If you possess the Sommerswerd, turn to **6**.
If you do not possess this Special Item, turn to **190**.

27

The stairs ascend to a chamber lined with wooden racks covered with saddlery, lances, tack and all manner of Kraan kit. A single Drakkar occupies this musty room. He is asleep on a chair near to a window which overlooks a landing platform and the city far below. You are tempted to take hold of the snoring guard and force him to tell you where Banedon is being held, but you daren't risk being detected. If the guard should raise the alarm, your chances of finding and rescuing your friend will be greatly reduced.

If you possess the Discipline of Kai-alchemy, turn to **282**.
If you do not, turn to **212**.

28

You land with a jolt that empties your lungs and sends red-hot pain lancing up your left leg. You have landed on a heap of broken bricks and rot-infested timbers, one of which has opened a deep gash along the back of your calf: lose 4 ENDURANCE points.

Winded, disorientated, and in acute pain, you crawl across the slimy floor of this cellar towards a flight of steps. Then, with a chilling suddenness, your senses warn that you are not alone. From behind, a lanky grey-skinned humanoid form creeps from a shadowy hollow, snickering evilly. It leaps upon your back and scratches your face with its razor-sharp nails. You twist yourself free and hammer your elbow into its chest, sending it sprawling to the damp ground where it lies deathly still. You draw your weapon and prepare for combat, but this proves unnecessary. Your blow has crushed the creature's brittle rib-cage, piercing its heart.

If you possess the Discipline of Deliverance, turn to **193**.
If you do not possess this Discipline, turn to **113**.

29

You dive to the floor and, although you avoid the full impact of the fiery missile, it glances off your right shoulder, burning you badly. Lose 8 ENDURANCE points.

If you have survived this wounding, turn to **167**.

30

Your arrow penetrates the beast's skull and kills it instantaneously, although the momentum of its attack carries its hulking body forward for several yards before it finally crashes snout-first into the iron drawbridge floor, and tumbles head over heels.

Turn to **213**.

31

Beyond the initial heaps of rubble this avenue is surprisingly clear of debris and obstructions. You are conscious that perhaps it is too clear, offering you no cover at all from the buildings which line this route to the centre of Kaag.

You decide to trust to the ruins rather than run the risk of being detected out in the open. However, within a matter of minutes you are confronted by a new hazard. The ground in this section of the city is unsafe. It is riddled with potholes and concealed cellars, covered by rotten wooden beams and slabs of paper-thin plaster. Suddenly one such section gives way beneath your feet and you find yourself falling head-long into coal-black darkness.

Pick a number from the *Random Number Table*. If you have the Discipline of Grand Huntmastery, add 2 to the number you have picked.

If your total score is now *0–5*, turn to **28**.
If it is *6* or higher, turn to **44**.

32

Arrows fly past you on all sides, forcing you to a halt.

''It's no good, Lone Wolf,'' shouts Banedon, as he watches the Drakkarim advancing along the passage, ''we'll have to go back and take our chances in the pen.''

Cursing your predicament, you turn around and hurry back towards the waiting ambush. You are expecting to be at-tacked by more archers, yet as soon as you set foot inside the pen you are confronted by something totally unexpected. A faint sound above makes you look up, and, to your horror, you see a weighted net falling from the ceiling directly on to your heads.

Pick a number from the *Random Number Table*. If you have Grand Huntmastery, and have reached the rank of Kai Grand Guardian, add 3 to the number you have picked.

If your total is now *0–4*, turn to **23**.
If it is *5* or higher, turn to **227**.

33—Illustration II (opposite)

Aided by your mastery, you traverse the tunnel without injury and reach the cooler section beyond. Here you happen upon a steep staircase, set into the right-hand wall, which ascends to a hall on the level above. This vault-like room

II. The skulls of rare creatures are displayed beside tanned hides, jewel encrusted bones and a statuette of Darklord Zagarna.

contains a wealth of grim exhibits, hung upon the walls and displayed in glass-fronted cases. The skulls of rare creatures are displayed beside tanned hides and jewel-encrusted bones. One item in particular catches your eye: it is a statuette, fashioned in the likeness of Darklord Zagarna.

If you wish to keep this Statuette of Zagarna, mark it on your *Action Chart* as a Special Item which you keep in your Backpack. If you already carry your maximum quota, you must discard one item in its favour.

To continue, turn to **178**.

34

Talons spring from the creature's forepaws and its sharp teeth glint like polished knives as it comes leaping through the air towards you.

Vodok: COMBAT SKILL 44   ENDURANCE 52

If you win this combat, turn to **130**.

35

As the last of the handlers falls to your deadly blows, his sword falls from his grasp and you notice a glint of polished metal, unusually bright, radiating from a chain bracelet dangling at his wrist. The source of the glint is a polished key fixed to the chain. (If you wish to keep this Brass Key, record it as a Backpack Item on your *Action Chart*.)

With the angry yelps of the Akataz echoing in your ears, you leap over the bodies of the slain handlers and sprint along the passage that leads away from the pen.

Turn to **262**.

36

You try to avoid being impaled upon the runaway log by diving between the spinning staves. You succeed in avoiding death, but one of the sharpened steel spikes gouges your leg, leaving a deep wound: lose 6 ENDURANCE points.

Adjust your *Action Chart* before turning to **182**.

37

You have only just re-entered the chamber when a second bolt slams into the floor of the tunnel. The blast and concussion throw you forwards, but you manage to recover your balance and stay on your feet.

The sound of the explosion revives Banedon and, although he is still far too weak to speak or walk, he manages to open his eyes and communicate with you telepathically.

"I know this chamber . . ." he says, *". . . I have been here before. Look there, at the statue opposite. You'll find a lever concealed at its side. It opens a hidden door. Hurry . . ."*

Guided by Banedon's messages you discover that there is indeed a lever as he described. You pull it and a panel in the stone wall glides open to reveal a secret alcove and flight of steps leading downwards. The sound of running feet warns you that the enemy are approaching along both passages, and so, without hesitation, you shoulder your friend once more and slip into the alcove to avoid them.

Turn to **188**.

38

After several abortive attempts to open the lock, you decide to abandon the door and leave the chamber by means of the narrow staircase. An unwholesome smell fills this dark spiralling stairwell and, as you descend, you are forced to cling to the wall to prevent yourself slipping on the uneven, slime-smeared steps.

After several minutes your painfully slow progress is halted by a huge mound of rubble. At first your heart sinks with the fear that you have reached a dead end, then you glimpse a pin-point of light filtering through the debris and at once your senses reveal that a chamber lies a few yards beyond. However, in order to gain access to this chamber you must first clear away some of the debris which blocks the stairs.

Pick a number from the *Random Number Table*. Now subtract 1 from the number you have picked. The resultant score equals the number of ENDURANCE points lost due to fatigue. (If you picked *0* or *1*, your score is zero.)

To continue, turn to **86**.

39

The psychic assault rakes your mind, leaving you stunned and shaky: lose 5 ENDURANCE points. Your Magnakai psychic defences rally to repel the probe and the pain recedes, but upon the instant that the attack is repulsed, the two dragon-creatures raise their scaly paws and shoot forth a stream of flaming bolts, aimed directly at your head and body.

If you possess the Sommerswerd, turn to **180**.
If you do not possess this Special Item, turn to **145**.

40

You sheathe your weapon and unshoulder your bow as you run towards the stairs. Once there, you draw an arrow and take aim at the advancing creature. It halts, snarling defiantly, then, to your utter amazement, its furry chest undergoes a rapid metamorphosis. What was fur only a few seconds ago is now a shiny steel-hard shell.

If you wish to aim your arrow at the creature's shell, turn to **10**.

If you choose to aim at its head, turn to **297**.

If you decide to abandon your shot altogether, you can shoulder your bow by turning to **108**.

41

As the Helghast closes for the kill it emits a wailing cry, sending a wave of psychic energy to assail your mind. Your Magnakai defences are more than sufficient to repel this weak attack and, to the creature's visible dismay, you remain unaffected by its initial assault. The Helghast's feral eyes blaze brightly and talons spring from its fingers as, with one last cry, it launches itself towards your chest.

If you possess the Sommerswerd, turn to **140**.

If you do not possess this Special Item, turn to **11**.

42

Wracked by fever, you slip reluctantly into a deep unconsciousness. Countless hours slip by while your body battles against the virus. It is a close fight but one that is eventually won thanks to your innate Kai healing skills.

Pick a number from the *Random Number Table*. Now add 3 to the number you have picked. The resultant score is equivalent to the number of ENDURANCE points you have lost due to the infection.

Once you have fully recovered, you pause to check your equipment before climbing the steps that lead out of this grim cellar.

Turn to **147**.

43

The moment you strike your killing blow, the body of the ice dragon becomes transparent, as if it was made wholly of glass, then slowly this form melts away to a steamy vapour which quickly evaporates, leaving no trace of the creature's existence.

A deathly silence fills the hall, broken only by the sound of Banedon's laboured breathing. Fearful of his condition, you climb the ivory staircase and rush to his side. However, you are prevented from touching your friend by the encircling wall of energy in which he is held prisoner. You sense that the power which keeps him here against his will is being generated by the crystal sphere which hangs suspended in the air directly above him. You gaze at this sphere and the thought occurs that if you could disrupt it in some way, by breaking or dislodging it, it might cause the power wall to fail.

If you have a Bow and wish to use it, turn to **211**.

If you possess Kai-alchemy, and have reached the rank of Kai Grand Guardian, turn to **60**.

If you possess Magi-magic, and have reached the rank of Kai Grand Guardian, turn to **94**.

If you do not wish to use a Bow, do not have any of the above skills, or have yet to reach the required Kai rank, turn instead to **292**.

44

As you fall, you throw out your hands and manage to grab hold of a thick timber which lies across the gaping hole. Splinters of rotten wood dig deeply into your hands, causing you to cry out in pain (lose 2 ENDURANCE points), but the discomfort does not cause you to lose your grip. With grim determination, you haul yourself out of the hole and continue across these perilous ruins, taking more care than before as to where you tread.

Turn to **147**.

45

The bolt strikes the pool and the inflammable liquid ignites with a deafening *whoomph* that knocks you flat on your back. For a few seconds the chamber is aglow with a blinding white light, then the glare fades to reveal the octopoid writhing on the floor, close to the blazing pool's edge, its loathsome body being consumed by a hungry mass of guttering yellow flames.

Covering your mouth with your cloak, you skirt around the burning carcass and approach the archway through the thick smoke. The sheet of blue-green metal that once blocked this exit is no longer there; it has moved aside to reveal a dark tunnel leading away from the chamber. Eager to leave this smoke-filled hall and continue your search for your captive friend without further delay, you hurry through the archway into the darkness beyond.

Turn to **171**.

46—*Illustration III (overleaf)*

You sprint across the street and bound up the tower stairs. You are halfway up when suddenly there is a loud *clunk*, and you look up to see a heavy wooden log, pierced by a criss-cross of metal staves sharpened at either end, come careering down the steps towards you. Frozen with horror, you can but stare at the brutal face of a Drakkar who is peering over the edge of the tower parapet. He guards this feeding tower and, with gleeful expectation, he watches as his "toy," the great spiked log, bounces on the steps and spins straight towards its latest unsuspecting victim.

Pick a number from the *Random Number Table*. If you possess the Discipline of Grand Huntmastery, add 2 to the number you have picked.

III. A heavy wooden log, pierced by a criss-cross of metal staves, comes
careering down steps towards you.

If your total score is now *3* or less, turn to **250**.

If it is *4–9* turn to **36**.

If it is *10* or more, turn to **300**.

47

"So we meet again, Lone Wolf."

The words, full of hatred, are spoken by a tall, ancient figure, whose gaunt face is framed by a shock of platinum hair. It is Arch Druid Cadak, ruler of Mogaruith, the leader of the Cener Druids of Ruel.

"What is your purpose here, Cadak?" you growl in reply, your weapon raised in case he or his minions should attempt to rush you.

"I am ruler of this city now. After all, is it not fitting that I should inherit the legacy of the Darklords?" Cadak's whimsical mood seems to change for the worse, a change reflected in his voice.

"Your meddlesome intrusions have cost me dear, Kai lord," he hisses. "We have a debt to settle and I intend to make you pay what you owe. I brought you here. It was my purpose. I have no interest in the inferior magic of this fool you call friend," he says, sneering at Banedon, "yet I knew he would be bait enough to lure you."

Slowly he steps towards the shadows and you tense yourself, fearing an imminent attack.

"Now you will settle your debt ... " he says, almost in a whisper, "once and for all!"

He snaps his fingers and you hear the creak of a heavy iron door slowly opening. Then a low, snorting noise echoes through the pen, stirring the caged Kraan and Zlanbeast to

sudden frenzy. You steel yourself and cast your eyes around
in a desperate attempt to see what it is that is responsible for
this sudden uproar. Then the cause emerges into the light
and your blood runs ice cold in your veins when you look
upon its terrible face.

Turn to **194**.

48

Beyond the west arch you discover a flight of stairs. Cautiously you ascend several levels of the citadel until the
stairs emerge into a vast, frigid hall which is festooned with
icy stalagtites. In the dim distance you see the yellowy glow
of a warmer chamber and you hurry towards it, taking care
not to slip on the treacherous, frost-covered floor.

You are near the centre of this chamber when the temperature drops dramatically. Unless you possess the Discipline
of Grand Nexus, you lose 5 ENDURANCE points due to the
extreme cold.

To continue, turn to **116**.

49

After a few minutes the tunnel ascends by steps to a cavern-
like chamber where the walls are mildewed and damp. A
sloping passage leads away to your left, descending towards
a distant pit which reeks of vermin and decay. You shun this
exit and turn your attentions instead to an iron door set into
the far wall. Although it is locked, you experience no difficulty picking it.

On the other side of the door you discover a torch-lit corridor leading off to the left and right.

If you wish to go right, turn to **218**.
If you decide to go left, turn to **146**.

50

Despite the fatigue of recent combat, you manage to erect a defensive wall around your mind which protects you from the Vordaks' attack. At first their destructive energy is absorbed by this barrier, then it is transformed and cast back at them with twice its original intensity.

The Vordaks reel under the impact of your psychic retaliation. Before they can fully recover, you run at them and launch yourself into hand-to-hand combat.

3 Vordaks (in psychic shock):
COMBAT SKILL 28   ENDURANCE 38

If you win this combat, turn to **225**.

51

The tunnel ends at a huge, echoing hall. It was once a place of worship dedicated to Zagarna, Darklord of Kaag. Now, however, it lies in total ruin, having been ransacked and destroyed by those who took command following his destruction, by your hand, at the raising of the Siege of Holmgard.

In the alcoves and grottoes that adjoin this hall, where once stood effigies of Zagarna, there now stand likenesses of Darklord Slûtar. Behind one such tribute you notice something very unusual, yet familiar. A column of shimmering blue light descends into the alcove from a hole in the middle of the roof and passes through a similar hole in the floor. Your senses tingle as you gaze at this column, for you immediately recognize its purpose. Within the confines of the light, gravity is greatly reduced. It is used as a means of transportation, an elevator that can take you to other levels of Kaag, either above or below. The last time you saw one of these devices was in Helgedad, the former principal stronghold of the Darklands.

If you wish to step into the transporter beam, turn to **110**.
If you choose to ignore it, you can leave this ruined hall
  by means of a tunnel in its north wall.
Turn to **220**.

52

You remove the item from the satchel and the two guards
scrutinize it. Then they nod their approval and draw back
their spears. At once the crackling crimson energy ceases to
arc between the shafts.

"You may pass," they say, without any trace of emotion,
and as they stand aside, so the two great doors glide silently
open. Steeling yourself, you stride towards the blazing purple light which fills the chamber.

Turn to **159**.

53

You unshoulder your bow, draw an arrow, and let it fly
towards the chest of the leading Xaghash. The shaft shatters
against the iron-hard scales which protect its heart, and
the great merciless beast roars with delight at your misfor-
tune.

Hurriedly you retreat, drawing a hand weapon in your defence as the two evil-eyed horrors come rushing forward
with murderous intent.

2 Xaghash: COMBAT SKILL 52   ENDURANCE 60

If you possess the Sommerswerd, double all bonuses it bestows upon you (for the duration of this combat only).

If you win the combat, turn to **239**.

54

Despite the treacherous condition of the tower wall, your natural skill and agility see you safely to the top. In less than a minute you manage to reach the level of the tower parapet.

Turn to **9**.

55

You enter the passage and follow it for several minutes before arriving at an empty circular room. The only feature here is a rusty iron ladder, fixed precariously to the wall, which ascends through a hole in the ceiling to a level above. There is no other exit from this chamber and so, with caution guiding your every move, you climb the rust-eaten rungs.

You rise through the hole to find yourself in a corridor which is strewn with human bones. Skeletons lie mixed in tangled heaps and many of the skulls and loose bones seem to have been gnawed. The psychic residues of pain and terror left by these luckless victims presses in upon your senses, making you feel queasy and claustrophobic. With pounding heart you advance along the bone-choked passage, stepping carefully through the skeletons to avoid making a sound. But you have taken less than a dozen steps when something unexpected makes you freeze in your tracks.

Turn to **186**.

56

You turn and enter a rubble-strewn alley which takes you deeper into the black heart of Kaag. A mile later you reach a broader street, partially submerged by brackish, ankle-deep slime. Beyond it, at a deserted square, you see a tangle of rusty iron pipes spilling out from a circular shaft in the ground. Jets of steam hiss skywards from a thousand tiny cracks in these old corroded conduits. Nearby, in the ruins, a guttering fire casts an eerie yellow light over the area. Shadows play upon the surrounding walls, cast not only by the fire but also by the winged Kraan which swoop back and forth across this square, dousing themselves in the jets of scalding hot steam.

You are watching the Kraan diving and twisting above the rooftops when suddenly your Magnakai sense of Divination alerts you to an imminent danger. You can sense the approach of a hostile creature, one which is using its psychic power to scan the surrounding area.

If you wish to avoid this creature by entering one of the ruined buildings that border the square, turn to **301**.
If you decide to hurry away from the square, turn to **4**.

57

You push down on the Zlanbeast's head and send it into a steep dive, a swift action which saves you from being knocked out of the sky by the cloud of deadly bolts. The streets of Kaag come rushing towards you with unnerving speed, but you control the winged creature skillfully, reining it in to level off in time to clear the ramparts of the South Gate. As you pass over this gate you catch sight of something strange yet wondrous to behold.

Turn to **302**.

58

You push aside the last remaining Drakkar and rush out into the passageway. At the far end you find a door which leads to a covered courtyard. A group of Drakkarim stablehands are sent sprawling as you career through them and sprint towards a low wall which encircles this part of the complex. Without looking back, you leap over the wall in one bound and race into the ruins beyond.

For over a mile you wend your way through derelict buildings before you happen upon an avenue which is surprisingly clear of debris and obstructions. You are conscious
that perhaps it is too clear, offering you no cover at all from
the tall buildings that line this route to the centre of Kaag.

You decide to trust to the ruins rather than run the risk of
being detected out in the open. However, within a matter of
minutes you are confronted by a new hazard. The ground in
this section of the city is unsafe. It is riddled with potholes
and concealed cellars, covered by rotten wooden beams and
slabs of paper-thin plaster. Suddenly one such section gives
way beneath your feet and you find yourself falling headlong into coal-black darkness.

Pick a number from the *Random Number Table*. If you have
the Discipline of Grand Huntmastery, add 2 to the number
you have picked.

    If your total score is now *0–5*, turn to **28**.
    If it is *6* or more, turn to **44**.

59

You hurry away from the dead Drakkarim and enter a tunnel
which is dank and humid. You have taken less than a dozen
paces when suddenly your senses alert you to a crude floor
trap. A pit of poison-tipped stakes, concealed beneath a large
square of oiled cloth, blocks the tunnel ahead. What would
normally have ensnared a lesser warrior causes you little
worry. With a single bound you clear the pit and continue on
your way.

Soon the tunnel leads to another hall, but the entrance is
blocked by a huge stone statue of Zagarna which has been
tipped on to its side. The statue must have shattered on
impact for the tunnel exit is almost filled with large boulders. In order to gain access to the hall beyond, you must
first clear away some of this heavy debris.

Pick a number from the *Random Number Table*. Now sub-tract 1 from the number you have picked. The resultant score equals the number of ENDURANCE points lost due to fatigue. (If you picked *0* or *1*, your score is zero.)

Turn to **86**.

60

You move back a few feet and raise your right hand, point-ing your finger at the glowing sphere. Then you utter the words of power that you learned from the man who you are seeking to set free, and at once your whole hand is encased by a crackling blue-white fire. A jolt runs the length of your arm and a bolt of energy leaps from your index finger to-wards the sphere.

If your current ENDURANCE points score is *14* or less, turn to **277**.
If your score is *15* or more, turn to **104**.

61

The leather Drakkar battle jacket and leggings fit easily over your close-fitting Kai tunic. The jacket has a large hood, with slits cut for your eyes and mouth, and you pull this down to cover your whole face. You stow your backpack in a canvas satchel and sling this over your shoulder before opening the door and setting off towards the distant thor-oughfare.

You stride boldly towards the two guards, hoping they will let you pass unhindered. But as you draw closer, they cross their jewel-encrusted spears to block your way. Raw power crackles like a sparkling crimson serpent where the shafts of the two spears touch, warning you that these are no ordinary weapons.

"What is your business here?" growls the guard on the left, his voice gritty and full of suspicion. "Why do you seek access to the Hall of Unholy Worship?"

If you possess the Disciplines of Kai-surge *and* Kai-alchemy, turn to **272**.

If you do not possess *both* of these Grand Master skills, turn to **22**.

62

An arrow gouges your heel and a sharp pain runs up the back of your leg, making you stumble. You struggle to stay on your feet but the weight of your unconscious friend throws you off-balance and together you crash down on the steps in a heap. The Drakkarim howl with delight and, as you pull yourself free, they fire a final volley of arrows.

There is a flash of light and a blinding pain fills your head, but this is soon replaced by a total blackness. You feel yourself falling forwards into an infinite void, as if you had just stepped over the edge of a towering cliff. Reluctantly you surrender to the sensation for it is the last you will ever feel.

Sadly, your life and your quest end here.

63

The weakest area appears to be the creature's throat, where the horny chest plates butt against the bony cartilage which protects its windpipe. You whisper a prayer to the god Kai to guide your arrow as you let slip your straining bowstring.

Pick a number from the *Random Number Table*. If you possess Weaponmastery with Bow, add 5 to the number you have picked.

If your total score is *8* or less, turn to **217**.
If it is *9* or more, turn to **198**.

64

You whisper the words of the Brotherhood spell *"Invisible Shield"* and feel a chill as some of your body warmth surges from your trunk towards your outstretched hand. Hurriedly you circle your palm in the air before you, barely moments before the Death Knights let loose a volley of deadly bolts.

Pick a number from the *Random Number Table* (in this instance, *0 = 10*). If you have reached the rank of Kai Grand Guardian, add 1 to the number you have picked.

If your total score is *2* or less, turn to **152**.
If your score is *3–5*, turn to **24**.
If it is *6* or more, turn to **296**.

65

Undaunted and undeterred by the charm that has been placed on this door, you settle down in front of the keyhole and set about picking the lock. More than once you wish that Banedon was fit and conscious; he would have no difficulty opening this door.

Pick a number from the *Random Number Table*. If you have Grand Huntmastery, add 1 to the number you have picked. If you have Grand Pathsmanship, add 2. If you have Telegnosis, add 3.

If your total score is now *3* or less, turn to **139**.
If it is *4* or more, turn to **261**.

66

The moment you land your killing blow, the Nadziran vanishes completely, leaving only a harsh, caustic stench to mark its passing. You sheathe your weapon and hurry through the open portal into a well-appointed chamber, its many tables and shelves filled with flasks, bottles and boxes of unique design. To your left you notice an oaken shelf sagging under the weight of three large, heavily bound books, and to your right there is a workbench stacked high with magical paraphernalia.

A search of this chamber uncovers the following items which may be of use to you during your quest:

Tinderbox
Laumspur (enough for 3 doses. Each dose restores 4 ENDURANCE points after combat.)
Vial of Gold Dust
Conch Shell
Silver Flask
Green Key
Brass Key
Copper Key
Rope
Comb

All of the above are Backpack Items. If you decide to keep any, remember to adjust your *Action Chart* accordingly.

To continue, turn to **286**.

67

Biting back your fears, you raise your weapon and focus on the advancing swarm. Suddenly your psychic senses tingle. These are no ordinary insects; in fact these are not insects at all. Your sixth sense detects that they are merely a clever illusion created to deceive you. Confident in this knowledge you stand your ground and allow the tide of creepy-crawlies to wash over your feet. Within a matter of seconds the insect horde fades and vanishes, dispelled by your disbelief in their existence.

Turn to **243**.

68

Upon the instant you strike your killing blow, the Korozon disintegrates. Within seconds, all that remains of this fearsome creature is a dusty, foul-smelling pile of dull grey tiles and shattered glass.

Covering your mouth with your cloak, you skirt around the remains and approach the archway. The sheet of blue-green metal that once blocked this exit is no longer there; it has moved aside to reveal a dark tunnel leading away from the chamber. Eager to leave this foul-smelling hall and continue your search for your captive friend without further delay, you hurry through the archway into the unwelcoming darkness beyond.

Turn to **171**.

69

As your final blow parts the head of the ghastly Vordak, it collapses at your feet and rapidly dissolves into a foul-smelling green gas. Mindful that the combat may have attracted others of its kind, you sheathe your weapon and escape from the area as quickly as you can. At the end of the street you see an avenue leading off to the south, and another, blocked by rubble, heading off to the west.

If you wish to follow the avenue southwards, turn to **123**.
If you choose to clamber over the rubble which fills the entrance to the west avenue, turn to **31**.

70

You utter the words of the spell *"Lightning Hand"* and point your right index finger at the creature's ugly head. You feel your arm tingling from the shoulder down, then a crackling mass of energy takes form at your fingertip. With a loud *crack* it arcs towards the oncoming beast and explodes full in its face, making it falter and cry out in pained surprise.

But it does not delay its advance for very long. Its horny eyelids save its sight and quickly it recovers, now more determined to fulfil Cadak's command. Hastily you draw a hand weapon as the shadow of the beast falls upon you.

Turn to **111**.

71

The tunnel descends, by slope and staircase, deeper into the bowels of the citadel. In the distance you see a torch-lit chamber and hear the sound of Giaks screaming in agony. As you draw closer to the room, your suspicions are confirmed that you have stumbled upon a torture chamber.

The Drakkarim torturers are too preoccupied with the mutilation of their charges to notice you slipping through their grisly workplace to the tunnel beyond. This leads to a large stairwell from where you can see many levels, above and below.

If you wish to ascend the stairs, turn to **126**.
If you choose to descend the stairs, turn to **92**.

72

After a hundred yards or so, the passage bears to the left then continues in a straight line until it arrives at a small stone-walled chamber. A crude cot, a chair, a battered trunk and a three-legged table made from a captured Freeland battleshield comprise its meagre furnishings. You stop to rest here for a few minutes, placing Banedon upon the cot while you half-heartedly search the trunk. Your curiosity is rewarded though, for inside you discover half a bottle of fine Slovian wine and a pouch full of Laumspur. You consume these (restore 6 ENDURANCE points) and, suitably refreshed, you shoulder your charge and set off along the passage in search of a way to escape from this dread citadel.

Turn to **251**.

73

You draw upon your skill and experience to mask your presence here in the ruins. The Vordak, using its psychic ability, scans the surrounding buildings yet fails to locate your hiding place. With a shriek of frustration, the loathsome creature turns and retreats from the square with its bow-legged Giak followers in tow.

If you wish to return to the street and continue your exploration of Kaag, turn to **123**.

If you choose to stay in the ruins and proceed in a different direction, turn to **31**.

74

Less than twenty yards ahead the street bears sharply to the right. You slow your pace and get ready to make the turn, but you are brought skidding to a halt when you see that the street goes nowhere. It is a dead end. A solid wall of black marble, thirty feet high, blocks your escape from the pursuing Death Knights.

Reluctantly you turn to face your foes. Having reached the junction and seen that you are trapped, they have spread out and are now walking slowly towards you in a line abreast. Casually they unshoulder their crossbows and prepare them as they advance.

If you possess the Discipline of Assimilance, and have reached the rank of Kai Grand Guardian, turn to **280**.

If you possess the Discipline of Kai-alchemy, and wish to use it, turn to **64**.

If you have neither of these skills, or do not wish to use them, turn to **133**.

75

Anxious to make up for lost time, you turn away from the altar and hurry through the archway opposite. Beyond lies an icy-cold corridor where the walls and ceilings are carved with many strange spatial designs. As you follow this passage, you notice that the theme of planets and stars gradually changes to one of volcanoes and lava fissures. As if to mirror this the temperature also changes, becoming steadily hotter and drier until, by the time you finally near the corridor's end, the heat has become almost furnace-like in intensity. Breathless and bathed with sweat, you stare through the shimmering air and see a great iron door at the end of the passage.

Due to the excessive heat, unless you possess the Disciplines of Grand Huntmastery and Grand Nexus, you must now consume a Meal or lose 3 ENDURANCE points.

Turn to **259**.

76

The flames lessen and, as the heat subsides, you lower your cloak and stare with trepidation at the sealed archway.

''He who does not serve . . . '' booms the voice, menacingly, ''shall not live.''

With a startling abruptness, there is a loud *crack*. Chunks of mortar fall from the octopoid mosaic above the archway and, to your mounting horror, you watch as the eyes of the creature begin to glow with a baleful green light.

Like a waking goliath, the mosaic comes slowly to life. Mesmerized by its pulsating gaze, you barely step back in time to save yourself when its tile-encrusted tentacles burst from the wall and come writhing towards your head. You lash out at the flailing limbs but your blow glances off the armour-like skin, inflicting no more than a scratch upon the tiled hide of this supernatural creature. The tentacles move apart briefly to reveal once more the two glowing green orbs. Then a wave of psychic energy buffets your mind, designed to weaken and subdue you, but your Magnakai defences deflect this attack. You sense that the creature is surprised by your natural resistance and, before it can muster its powers to launch a second, far-stronger psychic blast, you leap forward and aim a blow between its evil green eyes. You are within an arm's length of striking the creature's bulbous head when suddenly it squirts a stream of clear liquid from its beak aimed directly at your face.

If you possess mastery of Grand Nexus, turn to **121**.
If you do not possess this Grand Master Discipline, turn to **223**.

77—Illustration IV (overleaf)

You draw your weapon and steel yourself to fight the approaching beast. The boar-thing comes bounding on to the drawbridge, its red-rimmed jaws agape and its great curved tusks glinting evilly in the fires of the moat. Defiantly you shout your battle-cry and step forwards to meet its advance.

Gnagusk: COMBAT SKILL 41   ENDURANCE 45

If you win this combat, turn to **213**.

78

Using your Kai mastery, you focus upon one of the five feeding Kraan, the only one which is equipped with a saddle and reins. The other four abandon their feast and take to the air as you approach, but the target of your attention remains on the roof, cowed and submissive to your psychic command.

You approach this scaly beast confidently and climb into its saddle. Obediently it obeys when, with a kick of your heels, you urge it skywards. Its powerful wings bear you speedily towards the landing platforms situated high above the great north door and, as you fly closer to your destination, you see two which are open and unguarded. One has an arch-shaped portal, the other a wider, oblong-shaped entrance.

If you wish to land at the platform with the arch-shaped portal, turn to **105**.

If you choose to land upon the platform with the oblong-shaped entrance, turn to **244**.

79

The flaming arrow strikes the creature in the centre of its chest but causes it no harm. With a dull *crack* the tip snaps off and the shaft ricochets away. There is no time now for a second shot so you hurriedly shoulder your bow and draw a hand weapon ready. Sensing victory within its grasp, the creature emits a gurgling shriek and comes bounding forwards. You get ready to meet its advance but, when it is only ten feet away, it suddenly opens its mouth wide and spews forth a stream of white-hot liquid fire.

If you possess the Discipline of Grand Nexus, turn to **288**.

If you do not possess this Grand Master Discipline, turn to **248**.

80

You are within a few yards of the passage which leads out of the pen when suddenly the dogs begin howling in alarm.

''Intruder!'' screams one of the handlers, and points accusingly at your back. In an instant your weapon is in your hand and you spin on your heel, ready for combat.

The handlers jump to their feet and fumble for their weapons as they scramble to attack you.

*IV. The boar-thing bounds on to the draw bridge, red-rimmed jaws
agape and curved tusks glinting.*

"For Sommerlund!" you cry as they approach, then launch yourself at them in a determined counter-attack.

Drakkarim handlers:
COMBAT SKILL 35   ENDURANCE 39

If you win this combat, turn to **35**.

81

In a moment of vivid realization your Kai senses inform you that this creature is unaffected by normal missiles, yet it is specially vulnerable to fire. Hastily you replace your arrow in your quiver and search instead for something capable of igniting a fire.

If you possess a Lantern, a Torch, or a Tinderbox, turn to **191**.

If you do not possess any of these items, turn to **12**.

82

You draw your weapon and support your friend with your free hand. You tell him what you have sensed, that there is a strong chance that an ambush awaits you in the pen, but he agrees with you that a sudden rush towards the landing platform stands a good chance of success. Then, with a nod of your head, you indicate the Zlanbeast that is perched outside on the platform and whisper to Banedon that that particular creature is the one that will soon be carrying you out of Kaag. He nods his approval and you get ready to enter the pen.

You have taken less than five steps towards the platform when an unexpected sound makes you look up. To your horror, you see a weighted net falling from the ceiling directly on to your heads.

Pick a number from the *Random Number Table*. If you have Grand Huntmastery, and have reached the rank of Kai Grand Guardian, add 3 to the number you have picked.

If your total score is now *0–4*, turn to **23**.
If it is *5* or more, turn to **227**.

83

Using your skill, you will the gigantic Doomwolf to return to sleep. At first it tries to resist, but soon it succumbs to your psychic command and settles down to sleep once more on its bed of filthy straw.

Rather than attempt to force the door open, you cross the room and investigate its solitary window. It is criss-crossed with iron bars, but on closer examination you discover they are loose and badly corroded. A swift blow with the heels of your hands is enough to dislodge them, allowing you to escape with ease.

Turn to **284**.

84

Your throw goes awry. The weapon hits the crystal, but it only grazes its surface before falling to the floor. Cursing your aim, you retrieve your weapon and try once again.

Pick a number from the *Random Number Table*. If you have Grand Huntmastery, add 3 to the number you have picked.

If your total score is *4* or less, turn to **184**.
If it is *5* or more, turn to **224**.

85

After what seems like an eternity, the guards draw back their spears and at once the crackling crimson energy ceases to arc between the shafts.

"You may pass," they say, without any trace of emotion, and as they stand aside, so the two great doors glide silently open. Steeling yourself, you stride towards the blazing purple light which fills the chamber.

Turn to **159**.

86

Beyond the rubble you discover a large chamber fashioned from great blocks of polished blue-green stone. At the centre of this eerie hall there lies an oval pool of water, the surface of which appears to be alight with a myriad of tiny, pale green flames. The flames shed light on the surrounding walls but generate no heat.

As you approach the pool, you see a mosaic of glittering stones set high upon the far wall. They have been fixed to depict the shape of an octopus-like creature with two bulging eyes, a hooked beak, and twelve snaky tentacles. Directly below this mosaic is an archway which is sealed by a featureless sheet of solid blue-green metal.

Your senses tingle in response to the aura of magic that saturates this chamber. Fearful of what may lurk here, you unsheathe your weapon and hold it in readiness for your defence. For a moment the light of the pool flickers and the flames waver from side to side, as if disturbed by the passage of an invisible hand. Then, from the sealed archway, there issues forth a deep, resonant voice.

"Which Darklord of Kaag do you call master?" booms the disembodied voice. "Zagarna or Slûtar?"

If you wish to answer "Zagarna," turn to **136**.
If you decide to answer "Slûtar," turn to **173**.
If you choose not to answer at all, turn to **165**.

87

The Ashradon comes crashing to the ground with a tremendous noise. Its crumpled wings collide with one of the braziers, knocking it over and scattering glowing coals the length of the hall. One of these coals sets alight the sleeve of Banedon's robe, and you have to act quickly to extinguish the flames before he is badly burned.

Once more you heave your friend across your shoulders, then you hurry out of the hall and follow the tunnel for almost a mile before you reach a chamber where eight smaller passages disappear off in all directions. You scan these exits and a familiar fear returns to haunt you, a fear that you will never find your way out of Kaag alive.

Using your innate healing skills, you try once more to revive Banedon. You remember once, during a tutorial at the Kai monastery, that Banedon conjured up a vision of the monastery and its surrounding estates. You were able to see yourself in miniature, standing in your chambers as if you were a tiny animated doll in a doll's house. If he were able to perform that spell here in Kaag, you might well be able to locate your position and plan a route of escape.

Mustering your skills, you place your hands on Banedon's chest and transmit your power directly into his heart. (Reduce your ENDURANCE by 3 points.) Gradually he stirs to consciousness and, as his strength returns, rekindled by your healing power, he is able to grant your request. On the floor of the chamber he calls forth a living, three-dimensional vision of Kaag. Gradually this vision expands until you are looking at yourselves, kneeling on the floor of a chamber on one of the upper levels of the central citadel. The vision blurs and fades, but not before you are able to trace the quickest way out of this dreadful place.

The passage that heads due south from this chamber leads directly to the Zlanbeast pens and landing platforms situated on the exterior wall of the citadel, high above the great South

Gate. It is from here that you plan to escape, leaving the citadel the same way you entered it: by air.

Confident that the success of your quest is now within your grasp, you help Banedon to his feet and support him as you make your way along the south passage.

Turn to **231**.

88

To your dismay the arrow glances off the creature's tusk and arcs harmlessly into the air. With only seconds to go before the beast falls upon you, you drop your bow and reach to unsheathe your weapon. The bow tumbles off the bridge (erase this from your Weapons List) and you curse its loss as you get ready to fight to the death.

Gnagusk: COMBAT SKILL 41   ENDURANCE 45

If you win this combat, turn to **213**.

89

The stream of flame catches you full in the face and knocks you sprawling to the ground. Unfortunately your Magnakai skill of Nexus is not effective enough to save you completely from the effects of this super-hot fire: lose 8 EN-DURANCE points.

> If you have survived this wounding, you must face the creature; turn to **34**.

90

Expecting the unexpected, you enter a rubble-strewn alley which takes you deeper into the black heart of Kaag. A mile later you reach a broader street, partially submerged by brackish, ankle-deep slime. Beyond it, at a deserted square, you see a tangle of rusty iron pipes spilling out from a circular shaft in the ground. Jets of steam hiss skywards from a thousand tiny cracks in these corroded conduits. Nearby, in the ruins, a guttering fire casts an eerie yellow light over the area. Shadows play upon the surrounding walls, cast not only by the fire but also by the winged Kraan which swoop back and forth across this square, dousing themselves in the jets of scalding-hot steam.

You are watching the Kraan diving and twisting above the rooftops when suddenly your Magnakai sense of Divination alerts you to imminent danger. You can sense the approach of a hostile creature, one which is using its psychic power to scan the surrounding area.

> If you wish to avoid this creature by entering one of the ruined buildings which border the square, turn to **301**.
> If you decide to hurry away from this square, turn to **4**.

91

Aching with battle fatigue and the pain of your wounds, you stumble and fall to your knees before the mighty Zavaghar. Cadak laughs like a madman and screams for his creature to finish you off quickly. The beast rises up on its hind legs in readiness to strike you a killing blow, but suddenly, as it reaches its full height, its limbs and torso become stiff and its movements jerky.

"Slay the beast, Lone Wolf!" whispers Banedon, the words forming in your mind. *"I cannot hold it for long."*

You glance to where your friend is lying and see that his trembling hand is stretched out towards the towering Zavaghar. Inspired by his courageousness, you shake off your fatigue and rush forward to plunge your weapon deep into the exposed belly of the beast, striking it a mortal wound barely moments before Banedon's *Spell of Holding* fails.

Turn to **214**.

92

The temperature rises steadily the deeper you descend this flight of stairs, causing you to give thanks to your Magnakai Discipline of Nexus which is sparing you any pain or discomfort. The stairs end at a chamber constructed of stones which radiate a deep purplish light. It is furnished with tables, chairs, draperies and carpets, all of a similar hue.

You are crossing the floor on your way towards a tunnel-like exit on the far side, when suddenly a secret panel opens in the wall and from out of the darkness step two horny-skinned creatures which you recognize immediately. They are Xaghash, brutish lesser Darklords, implacable servants of the evil god Naar.

They are busily arguing with each other as they lumber into this chamber, and both of them fail to see you at first. But suddenly their senses detect the presence of your pure spirit, and it stirs them to a fearful fury. With frightening ease they hurl aside heavy furniture in their eagerness to attack you.

If you possess a Bow and wish to use it, turn to **53**.
If you do not, turn to **228**.

93

Your Magnakai senses warn you that the left road leads to a dead end. Without hesitation, you turn right and take off along the street at a steady pace. Although the Death Knights are hot on your heels, you are confident that you will soon out-run them. However, your confidence is severely shaken when you see that the way ahead is blocked by a hill of rubble, the remains of a collapsed watchtower.

If you have reached the rank of Kai Grand Guardian in the Discipline of Grand Huntmastery, turn to **19**.
If you have yet to reach this level of Kai Grand Mastery, turn to **199**.

94

You move back a few feet from the power wall then look up and focus all your attention upon the sphere. Silently you mouth the words of the Elder Magi battle-spell *"Splinter"* and, with a blink of your eyes, you project its energy at the centre of the glassy orb.

If your current ENDURANCE points score is *14* or less, turn to **20**.
If your score is *15* or more, turn to **256**.

95

Your Kai skills keep you safe from detection and enable you to cross the Akataz pen unseen. Quietly you enter the deserted passage beyond and press on with your search for Banedon.

Turn to **262**.

96

As you sprint towards the beckoning safety of the cooler tunnel section, you trip and stumble headlong to the floor.

Your hands and knees are burnt by rough contact with the red-hot metal, leaving them badly blistered: lose 3 ENDURANCE points.

When finally you reach the cooler section, you happen upon a steep staircase, set into the right-hand wall, which ascends to a hall on the level above. This vault-like room contains a wealth of grim exhibits, hung upon the walls and displayed in glass-fronted cases. The skulls of rare creatures are displayed beside tanned hides and jewel-encrusted bones. One item in particular catches your eye: it is a statuette, fashioned in the likeness of Darklord Zagarna.

If you wish to keep this Statuette of Zagarna, mark it on your *Action Chart* as a Special Item which you keep in your Backpack. If you already carry your maximum quota, you must discard one item in its favour.

To continue, turn to **178**.

97

You are struggling to recover your footing when you hear the metallic *twang* of a crossbow's drawstring, and feel something hard punch you squarely in the middle of your back. Fortunately, your Backpack has spared you from a fatal wound.

Driven by fear, you recover your footing and force yourself to the top of the mound. Only when you crest the summit and slide down the far side do you realize that the bolt has damaged one of your Backpack Items beyond repair.

Erase the item noted as No. 3 on your current list of Backpack Items.

To continue, turn to **291**.

You have only just re-entered the chamber when a second bolt slams into the arch of the tunnel. The blast and concussion throws you off-balance and, together with Banedon, you crash headlong to the floor: lose 2 ENDURANCE points.

The fall revives Banedon and, although he is still far too weak to speak or walk, he manages to open his eyes and communicate with you telepathically.

"I know this chamber . . ." he says, *" . . . I have been here before. Look there, at the statue opposite. You'll find a lever concealed at its side. It opens a hidden door. Hurry . . ."*

Guided by Banedon's messages you discover that there is indeed a lever as he described. You pull it and a panel in the stone wall glides open to reveal a secret alcove and a flight of steps leading down. The sound of running feet warns you that the enemy are approaching along both passages, and so, without hesitation, you shoulder your friend once more and hurry into the alcove to avoid them.

Turn to **188**.

You pull a wooden bung from one of the casks and cautiously sniff the contents. It contains a strong, foul-smelling spirit that tightens your throat and makes your eyes water, prompting you to discard it as quickly as possible. The boxes and sacks yield little of value; however, in one trunk you find the following items which may be of some use during your quest:

Rope
Lantern
Silver Bowl
Whistle
Brass Key
Black Key

Hammer
Enough food for 2 Meals

If you wish to keep any of the above, remember to record them as Backpack Items on your *Action Chart*.

To continue, turn to **192**.

100

The stairs seem to go on forever. You lose count of the number of levels through which you ascend and, after an hour of relentless climbing, you feel the need for rest and refreshment. Unless you possess the Discipline of Grand Huntmastery, you must now eat a Meal or lose 3 ENDURANCE points.

Eventually the stairs end at a tunnel which leads to a hall. However, you cannot enter this hall because it is blocked by a huge stone statue which has been tipped on to its side. The statue must have shattered on impact, for the tunnel exit is almost filled with large boulders. The thought of having to descend the stairs you have just laboured up fills you with dread, but in order to gain access to the hall beyond you must first clear away some of the heavy debris.

Pick a number from the *Random Number Table*. Now subtract 1 from the number you have picked.

The resultant score equals the number of ENDURANCE points lost due to fatigue. (If you picked *0* or *1*, your score is zero.)

To continue, turn to **86**.

101

At once you recognize the glassy orb which rests upon the altar. It is identical to the sphere you saw in the chamber of Arch Druid Cadak in Mogaruith, the sphere by which he communicated with the master of all evil—the evil god

Naar. With dread, you look upon the surface of the orb and your blood runs cold; it is as if the eye of the Dark God himself were gazing upon you.

If you wish to attempt to destroy this sphere, turn to **177**.
If you choose to flee from this temple as quickly as you can, turn to **75**.

102

You swiftly catch up with the fleeing Vordak and draw your weapon in readiness to cut it down. The creature glances over its shoulder and, as you strike out at its skull-like head, it raises an iron mace in an attempt to parry the blow. It manages to deflect your attack, but you quickly raise your weapon to strike again.

Vordak: COMBAT SKILL 22   ENDURANCE 28

If you win this combat in three rounds or less, turn to **69**.
If you win and the combat lasts four rounds or longer, turn to **246**.

103

As the last of the Drakkarim falls to your deadly blows, his outstretched hand grabs at your tunic and holds on with a vice-like grip. In order to free yourself you are forced to prise back the fingers one by one, mindful all the while of the Drakkarim squad who are arming themselves in readiness to attack.

As you disentangle the last two fingers you notice a chain bracelet dangling from the dead warrior's wrist. A polished key is fixed to this chain. (If you wish to keep this Brass Key, record it as a Backpack Item on your *Action Chart*.)

With the angry screams of the Drakkarim echoing in your ears, you leap over the body of the slain warrior and sprint along the passage beyond.

Turn to **262**.

104

Your spell causes the sphere to vibrate uncontrollably. Tiny cracks appear in its crystal surface then, with a flash of sparks, it breaks cleanly in two. At once the shimmering wall of light which imprisons Banedon flickers, then disappears completely.

Turn to **161**.

105

As the Kraan glides towards the semi-circular platform, you swing one leg over its neck and get ready to leap from the saddle the moment it lands. With cat-like agility, you jump the last remaining few feet on to the platform and run through the open archway. Two Drakkarim Kraan-handlers suddenly appear before you, but your quick wits and Kai camouflage skills keep you from being seen. As the handlers walk out on to the platform to tend to the screeching Kraan, you run towards the rear of the pen where a spiral staircase leads off to levels above and below.

If you wish to ascend the stairs to the level above, turn to **27**.

If you choose to descend the stairs to the level below, turn to **185**.

106

You rejoin your physical body barely seconds before the creature attacks, but the suddenness of such a swift transition leaves you trembling with psychic shock: lose 3 ENDURANCE points.

Shakily you draw your weapon as the boar-thing comes bounding towards you, its mouth agape and its great curved tusks glinting evilly in the fire of the moat.

Gnagusk: COMBAT SKILL 41   ENDURANCE 45

If you win this combat, turn to **281**.

107

Directly across the street from where you are hiding, you see a square, flat-roofed tower, one of several which encircle the outer edge of the concourse. A flock of screeching Kraan are feeding on slabs of maggoty meat which have been left there by the Drakkarim guards. Once they have eaten their fill, they take to the air and return to their cave-like pens, located high up on the citadel's outer wall. Some of the returning Kraan are ridden by Drakkarim and other guards who steer their mounts towards landing platforms which jut like great steel tongues from the entrances to the pens.

It occurs to you that if you were able to mount one of the feeding Kraan, you could attempt to enter the citadel by the very same route.

Emboldened by your plan, you resolve to put it into action. Patiently you survey the feeding tower opposite and note that there are two ways to gain access to its roof. You could climb a staircase that runs directly from the street to the roof, or you could attempt to scale its wall.

If you possess the Discipline of Grand Pathsmanship, turn to **204**.
If you do not possess this Discipline, turn to **129**.

108

Hurriedly you replace your arrow and shoulder your bow. Sensing victory within its grasp, the creature emits a gur-

gling shriek and comes bounding forwards. You get ready to
meet its advance but, when it is only ten feet away, it suddenly opens its mouth wide and spews forth a stream of
white-hot liquid fire.

If you possess the Discipline of Grand Nexus, turn to **288**.
If you do not possess this Grand Master Discipline, turn
to **248**.

109

The further you explore along this tunnel, so the sense of
impending doom becomes greater. Although the plain grey
walls, ceiling, and floor of this passage appear featureless
and ordinary, you are soon brought to a halt by the overwhelming presentiment of danger. Instinctively you reach
for your weapon, but before your hand tightens around it, a
slick syrupy sound draws your eyes to the arched ceiling
above.

Fear stabs like an ice-cold spike in your heart when you see
three jelly-like discs peel away from the roof and come
plummeting down towards your head. Each of the rubbery
discs has two sets of snake-like fangs which trail sticky
yellow venom. At once you recognize these deadly creatures: they are Plaak, live instruments of assassination employed by the Nadziranim.

Desperate to avoid their venomous fangs, you hurl yourself backwards and crash heavily to the ground. Breath-
lessly you unsheathe your weapon and get ready to
defend yourself as the loathsome Plaak bounce off the
floor and come arching through the air towards your
chest.

Plaak: COMBAT SKILL 39   ENDURANCE 20

These creatures are immune to all forms of psychic attack.

You may evade this combat after three rounds by turning
to **120**.
If you win the combat, turn to **247**.

110

You step warily into the glimmering column of light and
immediately feel yourself begin to rise. Bands of darkness flick past with growing rapidity, each one marking a
passing level of this mountainous citadel. Then you feel
yourself slowing to a halt. The column fades and you find
yourself standing on a metal dais in the centre of a domed
chamber. Ahead you see a great door, forged of Kagonite,
and beside it there is a narrow staircase leading downwards.

As you approach the door, you notice the lock which secures
it. It is inlaid with a series of numbers and, at once, you
recognize that they are component parts of a combination
lock. One number in the sequence is missing. By tapping the
correct number upon the blank square, you will cause the
lock to disengage.

> Study the following sequence of numbers carefully.
> When you think you know what the missing number is,
> turn to the page that is identical to your answer.

> If you guess incorrectly, or if you cannot answer the
> puzzle, turn instead to **38**.

111

With a manic cry, the creature lunges at your head in an attempt to impale you upon its shovel-like teeth. You sidestep the attack and lash out at its throat before it can dodge your blow. You strike and open a gash in the leathery hide, but it is shallow and does not deter the beast from launching a second attack.

Zavaghar: COMBAT SKILL 52   ENDURANCE 60

If, during this fight, your ENDURANCE score falls to below *12* points, do not continue the combat. Turn instead to **91**.

If your ENDURANCE remains at *12* points or above and you win the combat, turn to **214**.

112

You draw upon your Magnakai skill of Kai-screen to mask your presence here in the ruins, but the Vordak detects a mental resistance where there should be none. It shrieks an unearthly cry and at once the troop of Giaks respond by drawing their swords and charging towards your hiding place.

Confident of success, you emerge from the shattered building and challenge your enemy—six Giaks and their Vordak lieutenant—to combat on the street bordering the square.

Vordak & Giak patrol:
COMBAT SKILL 37   ENDURANCE 40

If you win this combat, turn to **69**.

113

A wave of nausea drops you to your knees and at once you sense that the ghoulish creature has infected you with a virulent virus, which passed into your body the moment it scratched your face. Hurriedly you draw on your Magnakai Discipline of Curing in an attempt to counter this insidious threat, but already the virus has spread throughout your bloodstream. Shaking and sweating profusely, you keel over and fall flat on your back as a second wave of nausea and weakness robs you of your strength to resist.

If you possess some Oede, turn to **264**.
If you do not, turn to **42**.

114

The arrow hits the centre of the sphere, but the shock of impact is not sufficient to dislodge it. The power wall imprisoning Banedon remains intact and you are forced to try some other way of freeing him.

If you possess Kai-alchemy, and have reached the rank of Kai Grand Guardian, turn to **60**.
If you possess Magi-magic, and have reached the rank of Kai Grand Guardian, turn to **94**.
If you do not have any of the above Disciplines, or have yet to reach the required Kai rank, turn instead to **292**.

115

Defiantly you face the Helghast, your weapon at your side. The creature looks upon you and sneers, revealing two sharp fangs which protrude from its lower jaw. It emits a chilling cackle, full of hatred and contempt, and its eyes blaze like hot coals as it confidently quickens its gait. You focus on its ghastly visage and muster all your strength to summon a pulse of psychic energy. The pulse forms an invisible ball of power which speeds across the hall and slams into the head of the approaching Helghast. The concussive force of this psychic attack lifts the creature bodily into the air and sends it tumbling, like some hideous rag doll, backwards into the flame-filled moat.

As the last shriek of the doomed creature echoes through the hall, the two Drakkarim stumble to a halt and stare down into the all-consuming fire. Nervously they glance at each other, fearful of suffering a similar fate, but years of fierce battle discipline soon override their anxiety and, like two automatons, they raise their swords and continue to advance towards you.

Drakkarim veterans:
COMBAT SKILL 30   ENDURANCE 35

If you win this combat, turn to **293**.

116

Soon you arrive at a circular chamber. There is a huge hole in the roof and another hole, equally large, in the middle of the floor. Carefully you approach the perimeter of this hole and stare down into a deep, dark shaft. It passes through countless levels of the citadel, below and above. The edge of the shaft is overgrown with ivy-like creepers, and a tangle of thorny vines hang down from the levels high above.

If you wish to climb these vines to another level of the citadel, above the one you are currently on, turn to **249**.
If you choose to ignore the shaft and continue along an adjoining tunnel, turn to **51**.

117

You utter the words of *"Counterspell"* and instantly the wall of crackling energy is dispelled. Moments later the Liganim wands explode with a tremendous flash, killing their wielders. Unfortunately for them, your counterspell reversed the latent energy of their wands, causing them to overload and self-destruct.

The noise of the dual explosions freezes the escaping Liganim dead in his tracks. He spins around in the archway, his ugly face transfixed into a mask of sheer terror as he watches you come racing towards him with your weapon poised to strike. The sight is too much for his weak heart which ceases to beat moments before you land your blow.

Turn to **176**.

118

You notice that only one of the five Kraan is equipped with a saddle and reins. You focus on this beast and use your Magnakai skill of Animal Control in an attempt to subdue it. The other four abandon their feast and take to the air as you approach, but the target of your attention remains on the roof, eyeing you nervously.

You have approached to within an arm's length of the reins when suddenly the Kraan takes fright. It beats its wings frantically in an attempt to knock you away, then propels itself into the air. You leap for its neck and hold fast as the spawn clears the tower and takes to the sky. Desperately you try to swing yourself into the saddle as the creature hovers haphazardly, fifty feet above the concourse.

Pick a number from the *Random Number Table*. If your current ENDURANCE points score is 20 or higher, add 2 to the number you have chosen. If your ENDURANCE is less than 10, deduct 2. If you possess the Discipline of Grand Huntmastery, add 1.

If your total score is now *3* or less, turn to **14**.
If it is *4* or more, turn to **215**.

119

The guard finally loses his patience. He draws his dagger and, with a lunge, he tries to slash open your satchel, causing you to pull away and draw your own weapon. The guard recognizes that it is not one that a Drakkar would wield, and instantly he shouts out in alarm: "Intruder!"

The two silver-plated warriors raise their spears and a blaze of sorcerous energy erupts simultaneously from their tips. Crimson fire lances towards your body to pierce your chest and abdomen, the impact knocking you headlong to the floor in agony. Biting back the pain, you stagger to your feet and retrieve your weapon in time to fight off the merciless guards. But the alarm has been raised and, within minutes, the thoroughfare is flooded with Drakkarim and Giak soldiers. You fight bravely and dispatch more than fifty of the enemy, but eventually your strength fails and you are overwhelmed and beaten by the denizens of Kaag.

Tragically, your life and your quest end here.

120

You break free from the combat and run headlong through the tunnel without looking back. The Plaak are incapable of pursuing you at speed and within minutes you have managed to leave them far behind.

The tunnel continues for several hundred yards before arriving at an empty circular room. The only feature here is a rusty iron ladder, fixed precariously to the wall, which ascends through a hole in the ceiling to a level above. There is no other exit from this chamber and so, with caution guiding your every move, you climb the rust-eaten rungs.

You rise through the hole to find yourself in a corridor which is strewn with human bones. Skeletons lie mixed in tangled heaps and many of the skulls and loose bones seem to have been gnawed. The psychic residues of pain and terror left by these luckless victims presses in upon your senses, making you feel queasy and claustrophobic. With pounding heart you advance along the bone-choked passage, stepping carefully through the skeletons to avoid making a sound. But you have taken less than a dozen steps when something unexpected makes you freeze in your tracks.

Turn to **186**.

121

You twist aside and the liquid passes over your right shoulder to splash, with a sizzling hiss, across the chamber floor. Droplets of the fluid spray your face and cloak, but your Grandmastery of Nexus saves you from being burned by this highly corrosive acid, an acid which would have instantly sealed the doom of a lesser mortal.

Shaken but undeterred, you scramble to your feet and face the octopoid once more, determined to defeat it in combat.

If you have a Bow and wish to use it, turn to **209**.
If you do not, turn to **164**.

122

Your senses tell you that you possess the correct key to open this door long before you have even approached the door itself. You retrieve the key from your Backpack, insert it in the lock and twist it confidently. The lock clicks open and you pass through into the chamber beyond.

Turn to **283**.

123—*Illustration V (overleaf)*

The avenue continues to a square where stands a massive horseshoe-shaped arch, crafted from dull blue metal which is engraved with runes and evil insignia. A score of battle-weary Giaks, some Drakkarim, and a Gourgaz are resting nearby. No guards have been posted around their makeshift camp and your arrival here goes unnoticed.

Beyond them, in the middle distance, you see the base of the great citadel. It is a truly awesome sight, a pyramid of jet-black stone which rises to a needle-sharp peak more than ten thousand feet above the streets of the city.

Soon a rickety wooden cart, drawn by two ugly, ox-like creatures in harness, trundles into the square. It halts and its Giak driver pulls back the tarpaulin which is covering its cargo, revealing haunches of grey-green meat stacked in a pile. Unceremoniously, the driver tosses them to the soldiers who devour them with obvious relish. It is an unwholesome sight, made even more so when you realize that what they are eating is freshly slaughtered Giak meat.

Turn to **216**.

124

Your arrow slams into the centre of the crystal and cracks it open. There is a flash of sparks, then the shimmering wall of light which imprisons Banedon flickers and disappears completely.

Turn to **161**.

125

The Gourgaz, followed obediently by his squad of ragged Giak warriors, crosses a mile-wide section of derelict buildings before entering a broad, clear avenue where there is very little cover. Unhampered by the terrain, you watch as they start to out-distance you, but you are not lured into following them. You decide to stay in the ruins rather than run the risk of being detected out in the open. However, within a matter of minutes you discover the reason why the Gourgaz took his troops out into the open. The ground in this section of the ruins is unsafe. It is riddled with potholes and concealed cellars, covered by rotten wooden beams and slabs of paper-thin plaster. Suddenly one such section gives way beneath your feet and you find yourself falling head-long into coal-black darkness.

Pick a number from the *Random Number Table*. If you have the Discipline of Grand Huntmastery, add 2 to the number you have picked.

*V. Battle-weary Giaks, Drakkarim and a Gourgas rest near the
massive horseshoe shaped arch.*

If your total score is now *0–5* turn to **28**.
If it is *6* or higher, turn to **44**.

126

You climb the broad staircase, ascending more than twenty levels. Your camouflage disciplines keep you hidden from the inhabitants of the citadel that you encounter during your ascent, but as you climb higher, you notice that these encounters are becoming fewer and fewer.

At the top of the staircase you are engulfed by a furnace-like heat. A deserted corridor extends into the distance, its walls glowing a deep dull red. Yet beyond this initial section you detect that the tunnel is far cooler.

If you wish to try to reach the cooler section of this tunnel, turn to **271**.
If you decide not to enter the tunnel, you can descend the stairs to a lower, cooler level, by turning to **21**.

127

The moment the heavy iron bridge crashes down across the moat you leap upon it and race towards the dais. But as you near its centre a wall of sparkling magical flame erupts at either end, sealing off both routes completely. In desperation you call telepathically to Banedon, hoping to awaken him to consciousness, but you are unable to make contact. Then, unexpectedly, your psychic calls are answered by a blood-chilling scream.

Horror floods your mind when you realize that the person on the dais is not your friend Banedon—it is a Helghast. As the creature rises and its features twist and distort before your gaze, you cast an anxious glance back across the bridge towards the great door. Standing there now are two Drakkarim guards with a slavering boar-like beast which is straining on its leash. Suddenly the magical flame vanishes and, with relish, they release the creature and send it bounding towards you.

If you have a Bow and wish to use it, turn to **289**.
If you do not, turn to **77**.

128

You have retreated barely a dozen yards along the passage when suddenly a troop of Drakkarim appear in the distance, blocking your escape. They howl like demons and unshoulder their bows as they come rushing along the tunnel towards you.

Pick a number from the *Random Number Table*.

If the number you have picked is *0*, turn to **238**.
If it is *1–3*, turn to **245**.
If it is *4–9*, turn to **32**.

129

You move stealthily to a new position, directly opposite the tower, and wait for the traffic of Giaks and Drakkarim to clear. The street is soon empty and you get ready to make your move.

If you wish to ascend the stairs which lead directly to the tower roof, turn to **46**.
If you prefer to attempt to climb the tower wall, turn to **240**.

130

Slowly a brooding, malignant vapour arises from the creature's corpse to hover in the air above it. You sense a powerful magical aura radiating from this sinister shadow and, as you back away from it, a mass of swirling sparks begin flickering at its core. Banedon calls for your help, his cry echoing faintly in your mind. You spin around and see him falling sideways to the floor of the platform, unconscious and unmoving. Fear runs cold in your veins, a fear that grows wilder when you glance once more at the hovering shadow, for now it has descended to the ground and from beneath its curtain-like base there pours a seething tide of black-bodied insects, some as large as mice.

If your current ENDURANCE points score is *12* or lower turn to **26**.
If it is *13* or more turn to **67**.

131

The fell creature pins you to the ground and you feel its steely fingers clawing at your throat. In sheer desperation, you twist and writhe like a snake to free yourself from its deadly grip. For an instant its hold falters and you exploit this weakness to the full. Swiftly you bring your knees up to your chest and kick out at the creature's midriff whilst holding firm to the neck of its robe. The Helghast is sent tumbling over your shoulder to plummet, head-first, into the flame-filled moat.

Open-mouthed, the two Drakkarim stumble to a halt and stare down into the crackling fire. Nervously they glance at each other, fearful of suffering a similar fate, then they turn and run towards the open chamber door. Determined not to let them escape, you give chase and catch up with them within a few yards of the entrance.

Drakkarim:
COMBAT SKILL 26   ENDURANCE 35

If you win this combat, turn to **293**.

132

The torch-lit stairs spiral down to a busy hall where several stairways and tunnels converge. You stay hidden in the shadows while you observe the creatures, mainly Giaks and Drakkarim, who are using this hall to move from one passage to another. All, without exception, are clad in uniforms which have been dyed a muddy shade of orange.

After a short while, the hall clears and you hurry across it towards a tunnel directly opposite. It is the only exit from the hall to have been ignored by the flow of traffic, and you choose it in the hope that it will be empty of guards. An archway off the tunnel reveals a chamber where the floor appears to be carpeted with a fine grey-green dust. Your senses tingle with a premonition of danger as you stare at the phosphorescent lichen clinging to the rough-hewn walls. The glow from the lichen illuminates several stout pilasters supporting the vaulted ceiling and an arched exit on the far side. The surface of the dusty floor is perfectly flat, undisturbed by tracks of any kind.

If you wish to cross the dusty floor and enter the archway opposite, turn to **260**.

If you choose to ignore this hall and continue along the tunnel, turn to **71**.

133

Coolly you face the advancing line of Death Knights. There is nowhere to run, and there are too many of the enemy to hope to avoid all of their deadly bolts. Upon their leader's command, the Death Knights take aim and fire, sending a dozen iron-tipped shafts whistling towards your chest. You dive aside, but even though your reflexes are lightning-fast,

two of the missiles penetrate your heart, killing you instantly.

Tragically, your life and your quest end here in the dread city-fortress of Kaag.

134

The moment you cease tapping on the lock, a powerful charge leaps from the surface of the door and explodes in your hand, knocking you backwards to the floor: lose 5 ENDURANCE points.

Banedon, upon whom you landed when you fell to the floor, is far from impressed by your display of mental arithmetic and he asks to be allowed to see the lock for himself. You heave him on to your shoulder once more and carry him to the door. Even in his weakened state it takes him less than two seconds to arrive at a solution. *"Seven"* he says, telepathically.

You apologize to him, then tap the lock seven times, secretly hoping that he is correct, for you do not relish the thought of receiving a second bolt from this door.

Turn to **7**.

135

The floor of the tunnel is gently sloped and, as it ascends, you notice the temperature steadily becoming much cooler. At length it opens out into a dimly-lit chamber where the stone floor is strewn with wood-shavings soiled by dung and dried blood. As you enter, you hear an inhuman snickering sound coming from among the maze of stout pillars that support the roof. The sound causes you immediately to draw your weapon; you have heard this cry once before, and although it was several years ago, you have not forgotten the creature who made it.

Slowly, from out of the shadows come three hulking beasts, their yellow cat-like eyes glinting malevolently. Your fears are confirmed: they are egorghs, massive wild bear-like creatures native to the stormy northern coasts of the Darklands. Stirred by the promise of fresh meat, they advance towards you and make ready to launch an attack with fang and claw.

If you possess Animal Mastery, turn to **200**.
If you do not possess this Grand Master skill, turn to **275**.

136

''Very well, minion of Zagarna,'' rumbles the voice. ''Display proof of your allegiance to your master and you shall be allowed to pass beyond this chamber.''

The echoing voice has barely faded when suddenly the tiny flames of the pool are transformed into a hundred roaring jets of white fire. A wave of searing heat forces you to retreat from the pool's edge and, as you cower behind the protection of your cloak, you try to think of a way to satisfy the voice's command.

If you possess a Statuette of Zagarna, turn to **290**.
If you do not possess this Special Item, turn to **76**.

137

The flaming arrow strikes the creature in the centre of its chest and punches straight through the iron-hard shell. With a look of pained surprise fixed upon its ugly face, the beast shrieks loudly and paws at the shaft quivering in its breast. Then its scarlet eyes roll back in their sockets and it crashes limply to the ground.

Turn to **130**.

138

You enter the nearest building through a stable door in the north wall. Inside, you narrowly avoid colliding with a

Drakkar warrior who is carrying two buckets of water, one in either hand. Your speedy reflexes, and your Kai camouflage skills, prevent this. They also prevent him from seeing you enter. You follow him and soon find yourself in a cavernous hall which is divided into scores of small pens. Each pen is barred with iron gates which keep secure the Doomwolves that are stabled within. You use your Magnakai skill of Animal Control to mask your scent, but even so, some of the larger Doomwolves are becoming noticeably restless in your presence.

You leave the hall by an archway which leads to a long, narrow passage. You have taken less than a dozen steps when you see a group of Drakkarim approaching in the distance. The passage is dark, but it is too narrow to risk hiding here; the Drakkarim would likely brush against you as they passed.

Looking around for a way to avoid them, you notice two doors, one on either side of the passageway.

If you wish to enter the door to your left, turn to **236**.
If you choose to enter the door to your right, turn to **210**.

139

You have been working on the lock for nearly twenty minutes when suddenly you hear the *clang* of an alarm bell. Seconds later a troop of armoured Drakkarim and Giak soldiers comes rushing into the chamber and spreads out in an attempt to surround you and Banedon. You draw your weapon and fight bravely, dispatching more than fifty of the enemy, but they receive a constant stream of reinforcements and, when finally your strength fails you, you are overwhelmed by the merciless denizens of Kaag.

Tragically, your life and your quest end here.

140

You unsheathe the sun-sword and hold it before your face. At once a golden halo of flame bursts from its polished blade, causing the Helghast to shriek in alarm as it recognizes the power you wield. It breaks off its advance and staggers back towards the bridge, desperate to flee its nemesis. Determinedly you chase after this evil being and, as it reaches the drawbridge, you come to within a sword's length of its spine.

"Die, foul spawn!" you cry, and with one fell sweep of your arm, you cleave the demonic creature cleanly in two.

The sundered halves of the Helghast fall from the bridge to be consumed by the hungry flames. Open-mouthed, the two Drakkarim stumble to a halt and stare down into the moat. Nervously they glance at each other, fearful of suffering a similar fate, then they turn and run towards the open door. Determined not to let them escape, you give chase and catch up with them within a few yards of the entrance.

Drakkarim:
COMBAT SKILL 26   ENDURANCE 35

If you win this combat, turn to **293**.

141

You move quietly to a new position, directly opposite the tower, and wait for the traffic of Giaks and Drakkarim to disperse. The street is soon empty and you get ready to make your move.

You sprint across the now-empty street and crouch at the base of the tower wall. The brick surface is plastered with powdery grey cement and, as you look up at the roof twenty feet above, you steel yourself for what could prove to be a difficult climb.

Pick a number from the *Random Number Table*. If you possess a Rope, add 1 to the number you have picked. If you possess the Discipline of Grand Huntmastery, add 2.

  If your total score is now *3* or less, turn to **219**.
  If it is *4–6*, turn to **169**.
  If it is *7* or more, turn to **54**.

142
You speak the words of the Brotherhood spell *"Levitation"* and slowly you feel yourself rising out of the pool of dust. The moment your feet clear the surface, you reach out, take hold of the arched entrance, and pull yourself to safety.

Your submersion has cost you your money pouch and one item from your Backpack, lost when you first fell into the dusty pool. Erase all your Gold Crowns, and the first item recorded on your Backpack Items list.

As the effects of the spell wear off, you leave this sinister chamber and head off along the tunnel.

  Turn to **71**.

143
The fireball skims your back before impacting against a distant wall. Your swift reflexes have saved you from injury but now you find yourself lying face down in the seething carpet of insects. You feel them creeping and slithering across your skin, then your psychic senses tingle with a

sudden realization. These are no ordinary insects; in fact these are not insects at all. Your sixth sense tells you that they are merely a clever illusion created to panic and deceive you. Confident in this knowledge, you get to your feet, ignoring the mass of creepy-crawlies that are attached in clumps to your body. Then, in a matter of seconds, the insect horde fades and vanishes, the illusion dispelled by your disbelief in its existence.

Turn to **243**.

144

You draw your weapon and hold it in your right hand whilst supporting your friend with your left. Then, with a nod of your head, you indicate the Zlanbeast that is perched outside on the platform and whisper to Banedon that it will soon be your transport out of Kaag. He nods his approval and cautiously you take your first few steps into the pen.

An unexpected sound makes you look up and, to your horror, you see a weighted net falling from the ceiling directly on to your heads.

Pick a number from the *Random Number Table*. If you have Grand Huntmastery, and have reached the rank of Kai Grand Guardian, add 3 to the number you have picked.

If your total is now *0–4*, turn to **23**.
If it is *5* or more, turn to **227**.

145

You throw yourself down to avoid the fiery missiles and the stream passes over your head, missing you by inches. They rip into a pillar supporting the tunnel ceiling, and sever it cleanly in two. Then there is a thunderous roar and, in the blink of an eye, a whole section of the roof collapses, burying one of the dragon-creatures beneath hundreds of tons of iron and stone.

For several seconds you stare at the remaining creature through a cloud of choking dust. Then, as if prompted by a silent command, you are both galvanized into action. The dust clears and a flaming sword appears in the dragon's paw. With stunning suddenness, it leaps forwards and lashes out with its fiery blade.

Nadziran (in dragon guise, with flamesword):
COMBAT SKILL 46   ENDURANCE 40

This creature possesses strong psychic ability. Unless you possess the Discipline of Kai-screen, deduct 2 ENDURANCE points every round you are in combat due to its relentless psychic assault.

If you win the combat, turn to **66**.

146

The corridor wends a tortuous route through a series of interconnecting caverns and chambers. Some are occupied by lowly Giak slaves engaged in menial tasks, none of whom notice your stealthy passing.

After nearly an hour you arrive at a large hall which is littered with stout trestle tables and wooden benches. A squad of thirty Drakkarim are seated around the largest table, hungrily devouring a foul-smelling feast of meat and wine. You note that most are unarmed, their weapons having been heaped upon an adjoining table prior to the feasting.

From the shadowy cover of an alcove you listen to their idle chatter, hoping to glean clues as to the location of Zagarna's courtroom, but, unfortunately, your patience goes unrewarded. These troops seem preoccupied with exaggerating the success of ambushes which they have launched recently

VI. The dragon leaps forwards and lashes out with its fiery blade.

upon their enemies in the streets around the citadel. However, from this barrack-room talk you do learn two interesting facts about the struggle taking place within Kaag. The two warring factions are fighting principally for control over the Giak spawning vats located in the dungeons of the citadel. The vats are the key to power here; they produce both an unending supply of fresh troops and a source of raw food for whoever controls them.

Anxious to continue your quest, you resolve to leave the hall by an archway on the far side. Although confident that your camouflage skills will keep you hidden from the Drakkarim, the hall is well-lit and there is a slim chance that you could be seen.

Pick a number from the *Random Number Table*. If you have the Discipline of Grand Huntmastery, add 2 to the number you have picked.

If your total is *3* or less, turn to **179**.
If it is *4* or more, turn to **222**.

147

Eventually you clear this section of the city and find yourself heading due south towards the great citadel. Soon the street opens out to a wide concourse which encircles the citadel and offers access to its great northern door. The entire door is made of black iron and is streaked with rust. Turrets jut from either side, on top of which are mounted giant cannonlike weapons, similar to those once employed by the Darklords aboard their ironclad fleets.

From the cover of a ruined house, you watch the traffic of Giaks and Drakkarim, all clad in orange uniforms bearing the mark of a bloodied scythe. The more you stare at the citadel, the more you feel sure that this is where Banedon is being held prisoner. However, entry into the citadel itself looks to be impossible, until, that is, an opportunity unexpectedly presents itself.

Turn to **107**.

148

The creature is less than ten feet away when it opens its mouth wide and spews forth a stream of white-hot liquid fire.

If you possess the Discipline of Grand Nexus, turn to **288**.
If you do not possess this Grand Master Discipline turn to **248**.

149

Your psychic defences repel the probe and the pain rapidly recedes. But upon the instant that the attack is repulsed, the two dragon-creatures raise their scaly paws and shoot forth a stream of flaming bolts, aimed directly at your head and body.

If you possess the Sommerswerd, turn to **180**.
If you do not possess this Special Item, turn to **145**.

150

The guards see the approaching clouds of smoke and immediately they come thundering along the corridor. You step away from the door, expecting them to kick it open and come rushing in, but instead they skid to a halt and hurriedly pull the door closed to stop the fire spreading into the corridor. They wait outside for several minutes before they are sure it is safe, then together they return to their positions.

Unfortunately your plan has backfired, but at least your Magnakai skill of Nexus enables you to extinguish the fire before it gets out of control. Frustrated but not defeated, you return to the spyhole and try to formulate a more successful plan.

Turn to **241**.

151

You enter the passage, but you have covered less than fifteen yards when you see something which forces you to a halt. A group of figures clad in hooded orange robes are walking towards you from the opposite end of the passage. The leader wears silver bracers on his wrists and he carries a silver staff which he levels at you the moment he sees you and Banedon in the tunnel ahead.

Instinctively you dodge aside; it is an instinct that saves both your lives, for without warning a radiant bolt of energy leaps from the tip of the creature's staff and comes hurtling along the passage to explode in the chamber behind. Hurriedly you turn and run from the group as the leader makes ready to launch a second bolt.

Pick a number from the *Random Number Table*.

If the number you have chosen is even (*0, 2, 4, 6, 8*), turn to **98**.
If the number is odd (*1, 3, 5, 7, 9*), turn to **37**.

152

Your hastily constructed shield fails to protect you against all of the speeding crossbow bolts. Two penetrate its weakened edges, bursting through with a splash of yellow sparks to bury themselves in your thigh and shoulder: lose 7 ENDURANCE points.

Biting back the pain, you wrench the bolts from your body and stagger towards the Death Knights, hoping to break through them before they have a chance to reload and fire again. The sight of you recovering so bravely from such a fearful wounding leaves many of their number staring open-mouthed with shock. You dodge through their line with ease, and by the time they realize that you have evaded them, and start to give chase, you have passed the junction and have recovered sufficiently to run along the street opposite.

Turn to **230**.

153

You call to mind the words of the Brotherhood spell *"Lightning Hand"* and point your index finger at the keyhole. Upon reciting those words a surge of power runs along your arm, culminating in a blast of energy that leaps from your fingertip and rips into the lock-plate. Some glowing splinters from the torn plate pepper your face (lose 2 ENDURANCE points), but your spell has worked: the door is now open.

Turn to **283**.

154

Beyond the archway, a passage leads to a pair of stout steel-sheathed doors. The lock that secures them is inlaid with a series of numbers and you immediately recognize that they are part of a combination lock. One number in the sequence is missing. By tapping the correct number upon the blank square, you will cause the lock to disengage.

Study the following sequence of numbers carefully. When you think you know what the missing number is, turn to the page that is identical to your answer.

If you guess incorrectly, or if you cannot answer the puzzle, turn instead to **257**.

155

Hastily you push Banedon behind you to shield him with your body as the Drakkarim come rushing across the pen, their barbed tridents poised to strike. "Taag!" they cry, and fall upon you.

Drakkarim:
COMBAT SKILL 34   ENDURANCE 36

Due to your need to defend both yourself and Banedon, reduce your COMBAT SKILL by 3 for the duration of this fight.

If you win the combat, turn to **278**.

156

Driven by fear, you recover your footing and force yourself to the top of the mound. The pursuing Death Knights, handicapped by their weighty armour and lack of special skills, can only watch in astonishment as you disappear from view.

The street continues beyond the mound, heading due south towards the great citadel, the shadow of this edifice looming ever larger. Soon the street opens out to a wide concourse which encircles the citadel and offers access to its great Northern Door. The entire door is made of black iron, streaked with rust. Turrets jut from either side, on top of which you see giant cannon-like weapons, similar to those once employed by the Darklords aboard their ironclad fleets.

From the cover of a ruined house you watch the traffic of Giaks and Drakkarim, all clad in orange uniforms bearing the mark of a bloodied scythe. The more you stare at the citadel, the more you are sure that this is where Banedon is being held prisoner. However, entry into the citadel itself looks to be impossible, until, that is, an opportunity unexpectedly presents itself.

Turn to **107**.

157

A ghostly mist issues from the parting jaws of the throne-statue. You step back, your weapon raised, but it does nothing to protect you from the piercing screech which suddenly fills your head. Fortunately, your powerful mind defences are protection enough against this violent psychic attack, and soon the screech fades to a more tolerable volume.

Turn to **253**.

158

Stealthily you tail the group as they wend their way through the alleyways and ruined streets of this quarter. Shortly they arrive at a complex of stable-like buildings, each one devoid of all decoration or embellishment save for a liberal coating of coal-black grime. Here the party splits into two groups. One section enters the complex; the other, led by the Gourgaz, continues on its way southwards, heading deeper into Kaag towards the sound of a distant street battle.

If you wish to follow the Gourgaz and his troop of Giak soldiers, turn to **125**.
If you choose to investigate the complex of buildings, turn to **138**.
If you decide to avoid both of these groups, you can make your own way deeper into Kaag by turning to **56**.

159

The purplish glare is generated by a glassy opaque sphere which hangs suspended above the doors. It pours forth a blinding curtain of light which fills the entrance, but this quickly fades once you have passed through into the chamber beyond.

As your eyes adjust to the gloomy interior, you find yourself standing in a small temple. A plain stone altar dominates the chamber, around which are positioned a ring of twenty black candles. The candles are fixed into elaborately carved holders fashioned to resemble each of the twenty Darklords sent long ago by Naar, King of the Darkness, to conquer Magnamund. Their flames burn brightly scarlet and they give off a rancid, greasy smell that, despite your attempts to block it, makes you feel light-headed and nauseous.

Hurriedly you dispose of the Drakkar uniform and move to leave this temple through an archway opposite, for there is an extraordinary saturation of evil contained within these walls and you feel it leeching your mental and physical strength. (Unless you possess Kai-screen, deduct 3 ENDURANCE points due to its insidious effects.)

You are near the centre of the temple when you notice something strange resting in a hollow in the surface of the altar.

If, in a previous *Lone Wolf* adventure, you have ever been to Mogaruith, turn to **101**.
If you have not, turn to **75**.

160

Your attempt to free yourself from your dusty entrapment goes awry. Your foot slips and your effort merely accelerates your descent. Within two minutes the fine grit closes over your head. You survive beneath the dust for ten minutes more before surrendering to your doom.

Tragically, your life and your quest end here in the citadel of Kaag.

161

You rush forwards and try to revive Banedon but he is deeply unconscious and does not respond. Taking hold of your friend by the arm, you lift him across your shoulders, then carefully begin your descent from the platform. Once you are safely at the bottom of the steps, you cast your eyes around the hall for a means of escape. There are only two exits visible: the light-filled doors by which you entered, and a tunnel in the north wall.

> If you wish to leave the hall by the main doors, turn to **172**.
> If you choose to leave via the tunnel in the north wall, turn to **268**.

162

You catch the fleeing Giaks and cut them down before they have a chance to retaliate. Breathless and bloodied, you are about to sheathe your weapon when suddenly you see the Vordak appear at the far end of the street. This time it is not alone; it is flanked by two others of its kind. With a chorus of shrieking howls, these three undead spawn raise their bony fists in your direction and launch a combined psychic assault on your senses.

Pick a number from the *Random Number Table*. If you possess the Discipline of Kai-screen, add 3 to the number you have picked.

> If your total is now *6* or less, turn to **274**.
> If it is *7* or more, turn to **50**.

163

A wave of negative psychic energy crashes against your mind and you stagger back, shocked and dazed by the ferocity of this unexpected assault: lose 4 ENDURANCE points.

> If you have survived this psychic attack, turn to **196**.

164

You draw your weapon but before you can raise it to strike, a mass of flailing tentacles come snaking towards you, forcing you to retreat towards the pool. Each of these limbs is tipped with a razor-sharp segment of tile which whistles as it cuts the air before your face.

Slowly but relentlessly the octopoid advances, pushing you steadily back towards the rubble-strewn entrance to the chamber. As it draws level with the central pool, you suddenly realize something that had eluded your senses when first you entered this hall. The pool itself contains not water, but a clear oily fluid . . . a clear oily *inflammable* fluid!

In a moment of vivid realization your Kai senses inform you that this creature is especially vulnerable to fire. Hastily you sheathe your weapon and search instead for something capable of igniting a fire.

If you possess a Lantern, a Torch, or a Tinderbox, turn to **191**.

If you do not possess any of these items, turn to **12**.

165—*Illustration VII (overleaf)*

The fading echoes of the voice give way to a low, rumbling growl which seems to emanate from somewhere behind the sealed archway. This rumbling persists for more than a minute until, with a startling abruptness, there is a loud *crack*. Chunks of mortar fall from the octopoid mosaic and, to your mounting horror, you watch as the eyes of the creature begin to glow with a baleful green light.

Like a waking goliath, the mosaic comes slowly to life. Mesmerized by its pulsating gaze, you barely step back in time to save yourself when its tile-encrusted tentacles burst from the wall and come writhing towards your head. You lash out at the flailing limbs but your blow glances off the armour-like skin, inflicting no more than a scratch upon the tiled hide of this supernatural creature. Briefly the tentacles move apart to reveal once more the two glowing green orbs. Then a wave of psychic energy buffets your mind, designed

VII. *Chunks of mortar fall from the tiled hide of the Octopoid mosaic as
its eyes glow with baleful green light.*

to weaken and subdue you, but your Magnakai defences deflect this attack. You sense that the creature is surprised by your natural resistance and, before it can muster its powers to launch a second, far stronger psychic blast, you leap forwards and aim a blow between its evil green eyes. You are within an arm's length of striking the creature's bulbous head when suddenly it squirts a stream of clear liquid from its beak, aimed directly at your face.

If you possess mastery of Grand Nexus, turn to **121**.
If you do not possess this Grand Master Discipline, turn to **223**.

166

Using your Magnakai skill of Animal Control you attempt to will the waking creature into returning to sleep. Unfortunately, this Giant Doomwolf is very hungry and it has already detected your scent.

Stirred to wakefulness by its gnawing hunger, and angered by the close proximity of a natural enemy, the great beast breaks free of the rope that is keeping it tethered and comes leaping through the air towards your chest.

Giant Doomwolf:
COMBAT SKILL 39   ENDURANCE 49

You cannot evade this combat and must fight this creature to the death.

If you win and the combat lasts three rounds or less, turn to **255**.
If you win and the combat lasts four rounds or longer, turn to **175**.

167

As the terrible pain in your shoulder subsides, you open your eyes to find yourself lying face down in the seething carpet of insects. You feel them creeping and slithering across your skin, then your psychic senses tingle with a sudden realization. These are no ordinary insects; in fact these are not insects at all. Your sixth sense tells you that they are merely a cunning illusion created to panic and deceive you. Confident in this knowledge, you get to your feet, ignoring the mass of creepy-crawlies that are attached in clumps to your body. Then, in a matter of seconds, the insect horde fades and vanishes, the illusion dispelled by your disbelief in its existence.

Turn to **243**.

168

Talons spring from the creature's forepaws and its sharp teeth glint like polished knives as it comes leaping through the air towards you.

Vodok: COMBAT SKILL 44   ENDURANCE 52

If you win this combat, turn to **130**.

169

When you are less than five feet from the roof, a part of the surface cement crumbles beneath your fingers. Desperately you throw your arms wide, seeking new purchase, and only just manage to prevent yourself from falling backwards to the street below. This close call leaves your hands skinned and bleeding: lose 2 ENDURANCE points.

Determinedly you haul yourself up the remaining few feet and take firm hold of the tower parapet.

Turn to **9**.

170

You draw your arrow and let fire at the creature's head, aiming for its eyes, but it twists its powerful neck as the shaft approaches and it lodges harmlessly between its teeth. The great jaw chomps down, pulping the arrow which it spits back at you with contempt. Hastily you drop your bow and draw a hand weapon as the shadow of the beast falls upon you.

Turn to **111**.

171

The dark tunnel descends to a titanic circular hall which is lit by a lava-filled vent at its centre. Tunnels radiate from this hall in every direction, like the spokes of an infernal wheel, their destinations mere pin-points of flame in the far distance. The air here is thick and cloying. It is choked by sulphur and other foul discharges of noisy engines located deep in the bowels of Kaag. The pressure of this tainted atmosphere is forever changing, causing you momentarily to lose your balance and stumble when first you enter the central hall. Before you, astride the vent, a colossal idol looms up against the crimson light like some supernatural giant forged of steel and stone. Warily you pass beside one of its huge, taloned feet, half expecting it to animate suddenly and come crashing down upon you as if you were a lowly insect. Fortunately, the foot remains immobile and you are able to leave by a triangular-shaped tunnel, the largest of those which radiate from this hall.

Other passages branch off this tunnel, spaced at regular intervals of one hundred paces. You detect movement taking place in several of these sub-tunnels and, when at last your natural curiosity prompts you to stop and observe one (using your Magnakai skills to magnify your vision), you detect that it is occupied by Nadziranim. These mysterious sorcerers are gifted in the black arts of Right-handed magic and, before their demise, they slavishly assisted the Darklords of Helgedad. These particular Nadziranim are busy at slime-filled vats, engaged in the harvesting of Giak spawn, a process that at first fascinates then rapidly repulses you. Sickened by what you have seen, you hurry away towards a distant junction where a narrower tunnel crosses from left to right. As you approach the junction, you feel the skin on your arms and the nape of your neck tingle with a premonition of peril. The sensation soon passes, but you are left with an awareness that a greater danger lurks somewhere nearby.

If you wish to turn left at the junction and continue, turn to **135**.

If you choose to turn right, turn to **109**.

172

As you are ascending the steps towards the curtain of light which hangs before the main entrance, your Kai senses warn you that there is danger ahead. You halt and listen. At first you hear nothing, then you detect the sound of marching feet. The sound stops and moments later you see the curtain of light shimmering; the doors to the hall have been opened.

Cursing your luck, you turn and run towards the tunnel as the first few soldiers of a Drakkarim patrol come marching through the light-curtain into the hall. They command you to halt but you ignore them and hurry across the tiered hall as fast as you can. Burdened by the weight of your friend, you cannot move as quickly as you would like, and before you reach the mouth of the tunnel the Drakkarim are taking aim at you with their bows.

If you possess Grand Huntmastery and have reached the rank of Kai Grand Guardian, turn to **2**.

If you do not possess this skill, or have yet to reach this level of Kai rank, turn to **233**.

173

"Very well, minion of Slûtar," rumbles the voice. *"Display proof of your allegiance to your master and you shall be allowed to pass beyond this chamber."*

The echoing voice has barely faded when suddenly the tiny flames of the pool are transformed into a hundred roaring jets of white fire. A wave of searing heat forces you to retreat from the pool's edge and, as you cower behind the protection of your cloak, you try to think of a way to satisfy the voice's command.

If you possess a Statuette of Slûtar, turn to **290**.
If you do not possess this Special Item, turn to **76**.

174

You reach to your belt and unsheathe the sun-sword. At once a golden halo of flame bursts from its polished blade, causing the Helghast to shriek in alarm as it recognizes the power you wield. It loosens its terrible grip upon your throat, enabling you to thrust the hilt of the Sommerswerd into its midriff and force it away. The Helghast emits a wailing cry and a wave of psychic energy assails your mind. But your Magnakai defences are more than sufficient to repel this weak attack and, with one fell sweep of your arm, you cleave the demonic creature cleanly in two.

The sundered halves of the Helghast fall from the bridge to be consumed by the hungry flames. Open-mouthed, the two Drakkarim stumble to a halt and stare down into the moat. Nervously they glance at each other, fearful of suffering a similar fate, then they turn and run towards the open door. Determined not to let them escape, you give chase and catch up with them within a few yards of the entrance.

Drakkarim:
COMBAT SKILL 26   ENDURANCE 35

If you win this combat, turn to **293**.

175

As the Doomwolf crashes to the floor, mortally wounded, you hear the sound of the door being unlocked. It is thrown open and in rush a group of grim-faced Drakkarim guards, their swords drawn ready for action. Swiftly you dispatch the leading pair, but more arrive to take their place, forcing you to retreat deeper into the cell.

Drakkarim Guards:
COMBAT SKILL 32   ENDURANCE 40

If you win this combat, turn to **58**.

176

You return to collect Banedon, then, once he is safely across your shoulders, you climb the stairs and hurry through the archway. A tunnel lined with rich wood panelling leads to a chamber where eight smaller passages disappear off in all directions. You scan these exits and a familiar fear returns to haunt you, a fear that you will never find your way out of Kaag alive.

Using your innate healing skills, you try once more to revive Banedon. You remember once, during a tutorial at the Kai monastery, that Banedon conjured up a vision of the monastery and its surrounding estates. You were able to see yourself in miniature, standing in your chambers as if you were a tiny animated doll in a doll's house. If he were well enough to perform that spell here in Kaag, you might be able to locate your position and plan a route of escape.

Mustering your skills, you place your hands on Banedon's chest and transmit your power directly into his heart. (Reduce your ENDURANCE by 3 points.) Gradually Banedon stirs to consciousness and, as his strength returns, rekindled by your healing power, he is able to grant your request. On the floor of the chamber he calls forth a living, three-dimensional vision of Kaag. Gradually this vision expands until you are looking at yourselves, kneeling on the floor of a chamber on one of the upper levels of the central citadel. The vision blurs and fades, but not before you are able to trace the quickest way out of this dreadful place.

The passage which heads due south from this chamber leads directly to the Zlanbeast pens and landing platforms situated on the exterior wall of the citadel, high above the great South Gate. It is from here that you plan to escape, leaving the citadel by the same way you entered it: by air.

Confident that the success of your quest is now within your grasp, you help Banedon to his feet and support him as you make your way along the south passage.

Turn to **231**.

177

You take up one of the heavy black candlesticks and raise it above your head, steadying yourself as you get ready to hurl it at the sphere. Then a wave of dark energy comes coursing from the orb and you swoon as it washes over your body. You are in danger of dropping the candlestick upon your own head until, with a defiant cry, you draw on your psychic strength to counter the power of the orb.

As your mind clears and your strength returns, you launch the candlestick at the altar and smash the orb into hundreds of tiny shards. Instantly there is a tremendous implosion and a rush of air as the evil within this chamber is sucked back to its source. The stench that permeated the air has now gone and you feel a sense of well-being infuse your body: add 3 ENDURANCE points to your current score.

To continue, turn to **75**.

178

You ascend several levels of the citadel, by slope and stair, until you reach a vast hall festooned with icy stalagtites. In the dim distance you see the yellowy glow of a warmer chamber and you hurry towards it, taking care not to slip on the treacherous, frost-covered floor.

You are near the centre of this chamber when the temperature drops dramatically. Unless you possess the Discipline of Grand Nexus, you lose 5 ENDURANCE points due to the extreme cold.

To continue, turn to **116**.

179

You are within a few yards of the passage that leads out of the mess hall when suddenly four Drakkarim turn a corner and come striding up the passage towards you. One of them sees you and shouts out in alarm: "Intruder!"

In an instant your weapon is in your hand, ready for combat. Behind you the feasting squad falls silent, then, as one, they jump to their feet and scramble to retrieve their weapons. Rather than face thirty Giaks, you decide to rush the four who are now striding along the passage, their swords drawn ready to cut you down.

"For Sommerlund!" you cry, and launch yourself at the four grim-faced warriors.

4 Drakkarim:
COMBAT SKILL 37   ENDURANCE 41

If you win this combat, turn to **103**.

180

You unsheathe the sun-sword and hold it before you. Immediately, the twin streams of fiery bolts are drawn to its golden blade. They hit the tip and merge into a searing hot ball of power which radiates a blinding white light. The

Sommerswerd vibrates in your hands. Desperately you fight to control the power that is held precariously in your grasp.

''For Sommerlund!'' you cry and, with a mighty effort, you cast the ball of energy at the two dragon-creatures. The meteor of light hits the leading creature and explodes with a brilliant flash. There is a splash of white-hot sparks and suddenly the tunnel is silent. The dragon-creature and the ball of fire have vanished.

For several seconds you stare at the remaining creature without either of you moving. Then, as if prompted into action by a silent command, the two of you are galvanized into action. A flaming sword appears in the dragon's paw and, with stunning suddenness, it leaps forwards into the attack.

Nadziran (In dragon guise, with flamesword):
COMBAT SKILL 46   ENDURANCE 40

This creature possesses strong psychic ability. Unless you possess the Discipline of Kai-screen, deduct 2 ENDURANCE points every round you are in combat due to its relentless psychic assault.

If you win the combat, turn to **66**.

181

The Helghast slams into your chest and drags you flailing to the ground. Frantically you try to get a firm grip on its robes as the two of you roll precariously close to the edge of the moat. With glee, the two Drakkarim stand back and watch your mortal struggle, confident that the Helghast will emerge victorious.

Pick a number from the *Random Number Table*. If your current ENDURANCE points score is 15 or higher, add 2 to the number you have picked.

If your total score is now *4* or less, turn to **286**.
If it is *5* or more, turn to **131**.

182

You race up the remaining steps and take hold of the Drak-kar by the throat. Desperately he fights to free himself from your crushing grip, kicking and scratching like a wild animal, until you are forced to let him go. As you do so, he stumbles and falls backwards over the parapet, landing with a shriek in the street below. You glance over the stone rail and see that he has met his doom, impaled upon the spikes of his cruel device.

Now you turn your attention to the five Kraan which are feeding on the roof. Gingerly you approach them, hoping not to startle them into flight, but the commotion, and your presence, has made them very uneasy.

If you possess the Discipline of Animal Mastery, turn to **78**.
If you do not possess this skill, turn to **118**.

183

You are unable to evade the creature so you raise your weapon defiantly and steel yourself for combat, as the shadow of this angry beast falls upon you.

Turn to **111**.

184

Once more your weapon hits the crystal and glances off without effect. You are moving forwards to retrieve it when suddenly the hall echoes to the clang of an alarm bell. Seconds later a troop of armoured Drakkarim and Giak soldiers comes streaming through the entrance and moves to surround you and your captive friend. You fight bravely and dispatch more than fifty of the enemy, but eventually your strength fails and you are overwhelmed by the denizens of Kaag.

Tragically, your life and your quest end here in the courtroom of Zagarna.

185

The torch-lit stairs spiral down to a busy hall where several stairways and tunnels converge. You stay hidden in the shadows while you observe the creatures, mainly Giaks and Drakkarim, that are using this hall to move from one passage to another. All, without exception, are clad in uniforms which have been dyed a muddy shade of orange.

After a short while, the hall clears and you hurry across towards a tunnel directly opposite. It is the only exit from the hall to have been ignored by the flow of traffic, and you choose it in the hope that it will be empty of guards. An archway off the tunnel reveals a chamber where the floor appears to be carpeted with a fine grey-green dust. Your senses tingle with a premonition of danger as you stare at the phosphorescent lichen clinging to the rough-hewn walls. The glow from the lichen illuminates several stout pilasters which support the vaulted ceiling and an arched exit on the far side. The surface of the dusty floor is perfectly flat, undisturbed by tracks of any kind.

> If you wish to cross the dusty floor and enter the archway opposite, turn to **260**.
> If you choose to ignore this hall and continue along the tunnel, turn to **71**.

186—*Illustration VIII (overleaf)*

In the dim distance you see a score of creatures stumbling along the tunnel. You magnify your gaze and discern that they are vaguely human in form, although hairless, lean and stringy as if from starvation. Their toes and fingers end in horny, hooked claws and their large eyes are deep set in skeletal faces, etched by untold years of pain and anguish.

You bring to bear your innate psychic skills and are shocked by what you discover.

Your senses reveal that these creatures were once human soldiers in the armies of the Freeland Alliance. Captured in battle and brought to Kaag long ago, they have endured unspeakable experiments at the hands of the Nadziranim. Now, no longer of use to those evil magicians, these pitiful victims have been left to wander the forgotten passages of this foul city, united in undeath.

When the undead soldiers are twenty yards distant you attempt to communicate with them telepathically. You sense that the one who is leading the group radiates a faint psychic aura and you hope that he may know the whereabouts of your captive friend Banedon. At first your questions elicit no reply, then, when your eyes meet, you feel a wave of despair wash over you as suddenly you tap into the agony of this creature's existence. (Lose two ENDURANCE points due to psychic shock.) As the effects of the shock fade, you hear a ghostly voice echoing thinly in your mind.

"Yes . . . I know of whom you seek . . ." it croaks. *"The Sommlending wizard is imprisoned here in Kaag . . . in Zagarna's courtroom . . ."*

You ask the wretched zombie for directions to Zagarna's courtroom but the only help he can offer is to tell you that it is *"many levels above."*

The pitiful group part in two to allow you to pass. As you move through them, your hatred of the Nadziranim blazes anew when you see upon the bodies of these once-human soldiers the terrible scars left by the cruel experiments. Filled with anger and remorse you hurry away, silently fearful that Banedon may already have suffered a similar fate.

Turn to **49**.

*VIII. Lean, hairless and stringy creatures stumble along the tunnel,
faces showing years of pain and anguish.*

187

The Vordaks cackle with glee at the success of their combined attack. Eager to exploit their advantage, they rush forwards drawing heavy iron maces as they prepare to finish you once and for all. As the pain in your head recedes, you raise your own weapon and get ready to meet their assault.

3 Vordaks: COMBAT SKILL 40   ENDURANCE 42

If you win this combat, turn to **225**.

188

The panel glides shut behind you and keeps you hidden from the enemy. Through the wall you hear cries of surprise and some curses when they enter the chamber to discover that you have seemingly disappeared into thin air. Mindful that they might find your hiding place, you descend the stairs and arrive at a vault which is lavishly equipped with all manner of elaborate laboratory apparatus. Several large tables line one wall, many stained with blood.

You sense that Banedon is disturbed by the sight of these tables and, when you ask him what is wrong, he tells you that this chamber is where the Nadziranim subjected him to hours of brutal interrogation in a futile attempt to extract the magical secrets of the Brotherhood.

"Despite all their fiendish tortures," he says, his mind-voice weak yet full of pride, *"they learned nothing."*

You search for a way out of this vault and soon discover a steel door which is secured by a curious combination lock. It comprises three raised blocks, each block divided into four equal squares. In each square, bar one, there is a number. You ask Banedon if he knows how the lock operates and he recalls once seeing a Nadziranim tapping the empty square several times in order to make the door open.

Consider the following grids of numbers. When you think you know what the missing number is, turn to the entry that bears the same number as your answer.

9	13
5	17

10	14
6	18

11	15
	19

If your answer is incorrect, or if you cannot solve the puzzle, turn to **134**.

189

Your arrow strikes the creature's head and gouges out a skull-deep furrow of skin and muscle before arcing away into the air. The beast shrieks with the agony of the wound and skids to a halt, twisting its head violently from side to side in a futile attempt to rid itself of the terrible pain. The wound has slowed the beast but not stopped it and, with revenge stark in its eyes, it resumes the attack.

Cursing its tenacity, you shoulder your bow and unsheathe your weapon in readiness for a fight to the death.

Gnagusk: COMBAT SKILL 41   ENDURANCE 45

If you win this combat, turn to **213**.

190

The fiery bolt continues to gather speed and energy as it comes racing towards you. It is barely an arm's length from your chest when you are forced to dive headlong into the insect swarm to avoid being hit. Pick a number from the *Random Number Table*. If you possess Grand Huntmastery, add 3 to the number you have picked.

If your total score is now 5 or less, turn to **29**.
If it is 6 or more, turn to **143**.

191

You hurl your light towards the pool and the inflammable liquid ignites on contact, with a deafening *whoomph* that leaves you sprawled flat on your back.

For a few seconds the chamber is aglow with a blinding white light, then the glare fades to reveal the octopoid writhing on the floor, close to the blazing pool's edge, its loathsome body being consumed by a hungry mass of guttering yellow flames.

Covering your mouth with your cloak, you stumble to your feet and skirt around the burning carcass towards the archway. The sheet of blue-green metal that once blocked this exit is no longer there; it has moved aside to reveal a dark tunnel leading away from the chamber. Eager to leave this smoke-filled hall and continue the search for your captive friend without further delay, you hurry through the archway into the unwelcoming darkness beyond. (Remember to erase the Backpack Item from your *Action Chart*.)

Turn to **171**.

192

Intrigued by the squealing, you approach the door cautiously and place your eye to the spyhole. Your fears soon melt away when you see two ragged-eared rats in a corridor beyond, fighting over a meaty bone. You chuckle as the smaller of the two unexpectedly wins the dispute and proudly drags away his prize. Your eyes follow the rat as it disappears towards a distant hallway where you spy something else that makes your pulse quicken in anticipation.

Using your Magnakai skills to magnify your vision, you see a pair of massive doors at the far side of the thoroughfare, guarded by two warriors clad in polished silver armour. A steady traffic of Drakkarim and Giaks passes to and fro before the doors, but none enter. You judge the hall to be over a hundred yards away, but even at this distance you can sense a great power is being contained behind the doors.

After a short while the traffic in the hallway subsides. Then two wispy, ghost-like figures glide into view, each clad in shimmering semi-transparent robes, and at once you recognize them to be Nadziranim—masters of evil magic. The guards step aside and, as the great doors part to allow the sorcerers entry, a flood of blinding purplish light pours from out of the room beyond. Suddenly your senses tingle with a premonition that your friend Banedon is close at hand. Convinced that you will find him somewhere beyond the doors, you resolve to gain entry as quickly as you can, but if you are to get past the two guards you must first create a diversion.

If you wish to start a fire in this storeroom in order to lure the guards away, turn to **232**.

If you wish to put on a Drakkar uniform (which lies

discarded on the floor nearby), then attempt to bluff your way past the guards, turn to **61**.

193

At once you sense that the ghoulish creature has infected you with a virulent virus, which passed into your body the moment it scratched your face. Hurriedly you draw on the healing power of your Grand Master Discipline and cause an army of antibodies to be released into your bloodstream to counter the insidious virus. You feel your temperature rise as the antibodies battle to clear your blood and, within a few minutes, this battle is won. The use of your Discipline costs you 3 ENDURANCE points, but it saves you from an otherwise grisly death.

Once you have fully recovered, you check your equipment before climbing the steps which lead out of this grim cellar.

Turn to **147**.

194—*Illustration IX (opposite)*

Emerging from the shadows with slow purposeful steps comes a huge rodent-like creature. Its mustard-coloured body and its six claw-tipped legs are thick and powerful, corded with muscle that ripples as it moves. Its head is monstrous, the jaw seeming too large for the skull. This entire bony structure extends beyond the lips and is studded with large spade-like teeth.

It turns its great head to look at you with cruel deep-set eyes and an eerie cry breaks from its maw. Cadak laughs with undisguised glee and, upon his command, the creature gathers speed and attacks.

If you possess a Bow and wish to use it, turn to **170**.
If you have Kai-alchemy and wish to use it, turn to **70**.
If you have Magi-magic and wish to use it, turn to **265**.

IX. A huge, rodent-like creature with monstrous jaw and large spade-like teeth emerges from the shadows.

If you have neither a Bow nor the listed Disciplines, or choose not to use them, turn instead to **183**.

195

You invoke the words of the Brotherhood spell "*Flameshaft*" and instantly the first few inches of your arrow are sheathed with magical blue fire.

Pick a number from the *Random Number Table*. If you possess Weaponmastery with Bow, add 5 to the number you have picked.

If your total score is now 6 or less, turn to **79**.
If it is 7 or more, turn to **137**.

196—Illustration X (opposite)

Swooping down from out of the shadows of the roof comes a huge gull-winged monstrosity. Its red reptilian skin is aglow with fine barbs, and a mass of coal-black hair streams from its bony skull. An open maw reveals a set of chisel-shaped teeth, many of which have been broken on the bones of past victims who have wandered unwittingly into this hall. It shrieks maniacally as it plummets towards your head.

You drop Banedon to the floor and unsheathe a weapon just in time to defend yourself against this creature's initial attack.

Ashradon: COMBAT SKILL 42   ENDURANCE 40

This creature is immune to Mindblast and Psi-surge, and suffers only half-damage resulting from the use of Kai-

X. A huge gull-winged monstrosity with glowing red reptilian skin swoops out of the shadows.

surge. If you choose to use Kai-surge during this combat, halve your normal COMBAT SKILL bonus for the duration of the combat.

If you win the combat, turn to **87**.

197

As you step away from the bodies of the two Drakkarim Death Knights, you notice they both have brass keys hanging on chains from their sword belts. If you wish to keep one of these keys, record it as a Brass Key in the Backpack section of your *Action Chart*.

A search also reveals the following items:

2 Swords
1 Dagger
Enough food for 2 Meals
80 Kika (10 Kika = 1 Gold Crown)
Bottle of Wine

If you decide to keep any of these items, remember to adjust your *Action Chart* accordingly.

To continue, turn to **59**.

198

The creature tries to sidestep your speeding shaft but it moves too slowly. The arrow penetrates the side of its neck, causing the beast to shriek out loudly in pained surprise. However, despite this fearful wounding, it does not break off its attack. With chilling disregard for pain it wrenches the arrow from its throat and hurls it aside. Unnerved by this display of bravado, you shoulder your bow as, with a gurgling shriek, the beast comes bounding forwards. You get ready to meet its advance yet, when it is but ten feet away, it suddenly opens its blood-spattered mouth wide and spews forth a stream of white-hot liquid fire.

If you possess the Discipline of Grand Nexus, turn to **288**.
If you do not possess this Grand Master Discipline, turn to **248**.

199

You claw your way towards the top of the mound, fearful all the while that you are presenting yourself as too easy a target for the crossbow-wielding Death Knights to miss. You are making good progress until, less than six feet from the summit, you slip on some loose rubble and fall.

Pick a number from the *Random Number Table*.

If the number you have chosen is even (*0, 2, 4, 6, 8*), turn to **156**.
If it is odd (*1, 3, 5, 7, 9*), turn to **97**.

200

Calling upon your Grand Mastery, mentally you command the three lumbering beasts to halt and, simultaneously, all three freeze in their tracks. Bewildered and frightened by the strange feelings that are coursing through their bodies, the three creatures back away into the shadows, whimpering grotesquely as they retreat like a litter of sick pups.

Immediately you seize the chance to escape and hurry past them, running through the chamber towards an open passage beyond.

Turn to **55**.

201

You summon forth the power word of the Elder Magi and direct it at the keyhole. There is a crack like thunder and the door shudders violently under the weight of its impact. A cloud of metal shavings wafts from the keyhole and, when you place your boot to the door, you discover that the spell has worked; the lock is broken and the door swings open.

Turn to **283**.

Drawing on your inner strength to quell your fears of what may lie ahead, you descend the ridge and approach the great, frowning bastions of Kaag. Through the swirling dust you see a pitted road which leads to the East Gate. Its storm-blown surface is littered with corpses, bleached bones, rusted weapons and armour. Crab-like scavengers scuttle among the debris, fighting for scraps to feed their young which nest in thousands of empty Giak skulls half-buried in the ground.

Shielded from detection by the storm and your Kai skills, you reach the breached east wall unobserved. Swiftly you climb over the rubble, which is heaped between the huge cubes of marble that once comprised this section of Kaag's curtain-wall, and find yourself in a street lined with decaying halls and slum dwellings. A dun pall of choking smoke hovers above this quarter, which reeks of iron and sulphur. Moving among the ruins you see a ragged group of Giaks, led by a Gourgaz clad in a shirt of mail. They halt for a few moments, then the Gourgaz hisses an order and they continue at a lumbering pace, heading south. You notice that their tattered blue-green uniforms all bear the emblem of a broken skull.

If you wish to follow these troops, turn to **158**.

If you choose to avoid them by heading in the opposite
direction, turn to **90**.

203

An arrow pierces your breeches and gouges a crimson line
across the back of your thigh, making you cry out in pain.
You stumble, but you manage to stay on your feet: lose three
ENDURANCE points.

Cursing the pain, you hobble into the dingy passage beyond
and descend by slope and stair to a rectangular hall which is
lined with ancient stone statues, their features made unrecognizable by age. Tar-soaked torches fixed to the two
longest walls illuminate this musty chamber with a flickering amber light, and the air is heavy with their oily stench.
In the distance you see an archway and the passage continuing away into darkness. Your injured leg aches viciously and
the thought of resting for a few minutes seems irresistable.

If you wish to stop here for a few minutes' rest, turn to **25**.
If you decide to press on without stopping, turn to **151**.

204

Your senses warn you that the tower stairs, although they
look empty, are in fact guarded by Drakkarim stationed
inside the tower. They offer the most convenient route to the
roof, but it could also be the most perilous.

If you wish to avoid the stairs, you can attempt to climb
the wall instead by turning to **141**.
If you decide to use the stairs, despite having been fore-
warned, turn to **270**.

205

You try to control your urge to struggle, yet you are aware
that even when you remain perfectly still you are sinking
little by little to your doom.

Suddenly the toe of your left boot strikes something firm and a shiver runs down your spine when you sense that it is a corpse. It is the body of a Giak who was thrown into this chamber as punishment for some minor infringement of citadel discipline. You wait until your foot is firmly placed on the corpse, then you tense your leg muscles and push yourself upwards as hard as you can, with your hands outstretched in a desperate effort to grab hold of the arched entrance.

Pick a number from the *Random Number Table*. If you possess Grand Huntmastery, add 2 to the number you have picked.

If your total score is *3* or less, turn to **160**.
If it is *4–8*, turn to **295**.
If it is *9* or more, turn to **8**.

206

The guards break off their conversation, then turn to face you once more.

"Show this relic," commands the warrior to your right.

Hesitantly you reach into the satchel and fumble with the buckle, stalling for time.

"Be quick," warns the other guard, reaching for a dagger with his free hand, "or I shall open it for you."

If you possess either a Statue of Slûtar, the Dagger of Vashna, or the sword of Helshezag, turn to **52**.
If you do not possess any of these Special Items, turn to **119**.

207

A sudden noise makes you spin around, half-crouched, your weapon ready to hand for your defence. At first you see nothing, then a faint shadow moving at the corner of your eye draws your attention to an alcove on the other side of the hall. Suddenly you hear Banedon's voice echoing faintly in your head. You cannot understand what he is saying but you sense that it is a warning. You glance over your shoulder and notice that he is pointing at the granite throne. To your horror you see that the throne's fanged mouth is opening wider and wider.

If you possess Kai-surge, turn to **157**.
If you do not possess this Discipline, turn to **229**.

208

You charge through the power-wall and your senses reel as your body earths the electrical energy: lose 3 ENDURANCE points. But, despite the momentary pain, you quickly recover and dispatch the two wand-wielding liganim before they, too, attempt to run from the library.

The noise of their dying screams freezes the escaping liganim dead in his tracks. He spins around in the archway, his ugly face transfixed into a mask of sheer terror as he watches you come racing towards him with your weapon poised to strike. However, the sight is too much for his weak heart which ceases to beat moments before you land your blow.

Turn to **176**.

209

You draw an arrow but before you can place it to your bow, a mass of flailing tentacles come snaking towards you, forcing you to retreat towards the pool. Each of these limbs is tipped with a razor-sharp segment of tile which whistles as it cuts the air before your face.

Slowly but relentlessly the octopoid advances, pushing you steadily back towards the rubble-strewn entrance to the chamber. As it draws level with the central pool, you suddenly realize something that had eluded your senses when first you entered this hall. The pool itself contains not water, but a clear oily fluid . . . a clear oily inflammable fluid!

If you possess Kai-alchemy, turn to **298**.
If you do not possess mastery of this Discipline, turn instead to **81**.

210

You pull open a bolt which secures the door and slip inside the room beyond. With bated breath you close the door and listen intently to the footfalls of the approaching Drakkarim, silently praying that they will pass by without checking this room. The steps grow louder, then, to your dismay, they halt immediately outside the door. You hear a gruff voice cursing, then there is a metallic click as the bolt is drawn. Unwittingly they have locked you in.

The Drakkarim continue on their way and you hear the sound of their heavy iron-shod boots receding along the passageway. Suddenly, a low growl makes you spin around, your hand flashing to the hilt of your weapon. Before you, resting on a bed of mouldy straw, lies the largest Doomwolf you have ever seen. It twitches and flicks its massive head as slowly it stirs from sleep.

If you possess the Discipline of Animal Mastery, turn to **83**.
If you do not possess mastery of this Discipline, turn to **166**.

211

You step back a few paces and take aim with your bow at the centre of the crystal sphere. For someone of your ability this is a target that is difficult to miss. But will the arrow strike with sufficient force to break or dislodge the sphere?

Pick a number from the *Random Number Table*.

If the number you have picked is *0–4*, turn to **114**.
If it is *5–9*, turn to **124**.

212

After some deliberation, you decide to let the Drakkar sleep on undisturbed. You climb the stairs and emerge in the centre of a hall on the level above. This vault-like room contains a wealth of grim exhibits, hung upon the walls and displayed in glass-fronted cases. The skulls of rare creatures are displayed beside tanned hides and jewel-encrusted bones. One item in particular catches your eye: it is a statuette, fashioned in the likeness of Darklord Zagarna.

If you wish to keep this Statuette of Zagarna, mark it on your *Action Chart* as a Special Item which you keep in your Backpack. If you already carry your maximum quota, you must discard one item in its favour.

To continue, turn to **178**.

213

You watch as the body of the slain Gnagusk slowly rolls off the drawbridge and plummets into the flaming moat. This victory fills you with renewed confidence, but the feeling is all too short-lived. Suddenly, two steely hands fix themselves around your throat, crushing your windpipe. The Helghast is attacking you from behind and, as you struggle to break free, its iron-hard fingers close ever tighter: lose 4 ENDURANCE points.

The two Drakkarim cackle at your plight as they approach the drawbridge, their swords drawn ready to avenge the death of their pet.

If you possess the Sommerswerd, turn to **174**.
If you do not possess this Special Item, turn to **252**.

214

214

The Zavaghar shrieks in agony and comes crashing to the floor, its limbs flailing and its jaw chattering wildly as it eeks out the last throes of death.

"No! No! No!" screams Arch Druid Cadak, his voice filled with anger and bitter frustration. "It cannot be! It cannot be!"

Madly he rushes across the pen and stares with open-mouthed incredulity at the carcass of the huge Zavaghar, his eyes wide with disbelief. Meanwhile, you have helped Banedon to his feet and the two of you have begun to hurry towards your means of escape which is still perched on the landing platform. Suddenly, Cadak recovers from his shock and, seeing the two of you escaping, screams an order to his remaining Drakkarim to prevent you from getting away.

You reach the winged creature and, using your Magnakai skills, you manage to subdue it to your command. Arrows and crossbow bolts fly past, dangerously close, fired by those Drakkarim who have responded to Cadak's order. You try to ignore these missiles as you mount the Zlanbeast and heave Banedon roughly across its great scaly neck.

With a sharp kick, you urge the Zlanbeast into the air and, as it soars away from the platform, you glance back to see Cadak shaking his fist and screaming vile curses.

You laugh at his displeasure, but your laughter chokes in your throat when you notice a battery of heavy bolt-throwers lining the battlements above the pens. They are manned by Giak soldiers, and, as you fly past them, they discharge a cloud of deadly missiles.

Pick a number from the *Random Number Table*.

If the number you have picked is *0–8*, turn to **57**.
If it is *9*, turn to **294**.

215
Using all your strength, you haul yourself into the saddle and hold fast as the Kraan soars upwards into the stormy sky. Frantically you kick and beat the creature with your fists until, reluctantly, it submits to your will.

Pulling back on the reins, you urge it to go higher. Then a few well-aimed slaps to its horny head persuade it to bear you towards the landing platforms situated above the great North Door. As you draw closer to your chosen destination, you see two platforms which are open and unguarded. One has an arch-shaped portal; the other a wider, oblong-shaped entrance.

If you wish to land at the platform with the arch-shaped portal, turn to **105**.
If you choose to land upon the platform with the oblong-shaped entrance, turn to **244**.

216
The troops have almost finished their grisly meal when a figure, clad in flowing grey robes and a helm of brightly

polished steel, swoops down from out of the brooding sky upon the back of a Zlanbeast. He screams orders to the Gourgaz who immediately responds by cursing and slapping his tired troops into line. The grey rider berates the sorry-looking squad before finally taking to the skies once more. Stung into action by his harsh words, the Gourgaz officer leads his unit away at the double.

Curiosity prompts you to follow them, although you take care to remain hidden from view. They zig-zag through a maze of back streets before arriving at the approach road to a large hall. Here a pitched battle is taking place between two warring factions: one side wearing uniforms of orange cloth, the other clad in blue-green.

For several minutes you observe the carnage taking place as the two groups fight for control of the hall. The fighting soon escalates to the surrounding ruins and wisely you decide it best to leave this area before you, too, become caught up in the fighting.

You notice a road away to your right which leads directly to the citadel. It is virtually deserted and seems to offer the best escape route from the battle zone. However, you have covered barely a hundred yards when you are suddenly confronted by a unit of Drakkarim Death Knights, reinforcements freshly arrived from the citadel itself.

Quickly you dive into a side street and run as fast as you can, but the Death Knights have seen you and, despite their heavy armour, they give chase determinedly.

The street soon ends at a junction where two roads branch away, one to the left, the other to the right.

If you have the Discipline of Grand Huntmastery, turn to **93**.

If you do not possess this skill or do not wish to use it, you
can take either the left road, by turning to **74**.
Or the right road, by turning to **230**.

217

The fiery arrow strikes the creature's throat but fails to
penetrate. With a high-pitched whine, the steel-tipped shaft
ricochets harmlessly away into the hall. There is no time
now for a second shot so you hurriedly shoulder your bow
and draw a hand weapon ready. Sensing victory within its
grasp, the creature emits a gurgling shriek and comes bounding forwards. You get set to meet its advance, yet, when it
is only ten feet away, it suddenly opens its mouth wide and
spews forth a stream of white-hot liquid fire.

If you possess the Discipline of Grand Nexus, turn to **288**.
If you do not possess this Grand Master Discipline, turn
to **248**.

218

The corridor passes through a series of interconnecting caverns, some of which are occupied by lowly Giak slaves
engaged in menial tasks, none of whom notice your stealthy
passing. After almost an hour, you arrive at a cavernous hall
filled with iron cages in which lie countless Akataz, a breed
of leathery war-dogs used by the Drakkarim. Nearby are a
group of Drakkarim handlers seated at a table playing cards.

From the shadows you listen to their idle chatter, hoping to
glean clues as to the location of Zagarna's courtroom, but,
unfortunately, your patience goes unrewarded. These brutish
humanoids seem preoccupied with their game, and the un-
fairness of their duties here in the Akataz pen. However,
from their banal conversation you do learn two interesting
facts about the struggle taking place within Kaag. The two
warring factions are fighting principally for control over the
Giak spawning vats located in the dungeons of this citadel.
The vats are the key to power here; they produce both an

unending supply of fresh troops and a ready source of raw food for whoever controls them.

Anxious to continue your quest, you resolve to leave the pen by an archway on the far side. Although confident that your camouflage skills will keep you hidden from the Drakkarim, the hall is full of keen-nosed war-dogs.

Pick a number from the *Random Number Table*. If you have the Discipline of Grand Huntmastery, add 2 to the number you have picked.

If your total is *4* or less, turn to **80**.
If it is *5* or more, turn to **95**.

219

You are within a few feet of the roof when a part of the surface cement crumbles beneath your fingers. You try to reach up and find new purchase but it is too late; you are already falling backwards to the street below.

On landing you strike your head and lose consciousness. Tragically you never reawaken. Your body is discovered by a Giak patrol who kill you out of hand, thinking you to be an enemy Drakkar spy in disguise.

Your life and your quest end here in Kaag.

220

The tunnel leads to another hall, but the entrance is blocked by a huge stone statue of Zagarna which has been tipped on to its side. The statue must have shattered on impact for the tunnel exit is almost filled with large boulders. In order to gain access to the hall beyond, you must first clear away some of this heavy debris.

Pick a number from the *Random Number Table*. Now subtract 1 from the number you have picked.

The resultant score equals the number of ENDURANCE points lost due to fatigue. (If you picked *0 or 1*, your score is zero.)

To continue, turn to **86**.

221

You examine the door more closely and soon discover it is locked, held secure by a common deadlock. Confidently you call upon your Magnakai skill of Nexus in an attempt to pick this lock, but to your dismay, you cannot cause the mechanism to disengage. A magical charm has been placed upon this door, making the lock pick-proof.

If you possess Kai-alchemy, and wish to use it, turn to **153**.

If you possess Magi-magic, and wish to use it, turn to **201**.

If you have neither of these Disciplines, or choose not to use them, turn to **65**.

222

You are within a few yards of the passage that leads out of the mess hall when suddenly four Drakkarim turn a corner and come striding up the passage towards you. Hurriedly you flatten yourself against the nearest wall and muster your Kai camouflage skills in an attempt to stay hidden.

The four stride past within an arm's length of your position yet they fail to detect your presence. Once they are inside the hall you peel yourself away from the wall and quickly escape into the passage.

Turn to **262**.

223

You twist aside in time to avoid the liquid, but a small quantity still splashes your right shoulder and cheek. Instantly there is a sizzling hiss and you feel a searing pain engulf your head and upper body as this highly corrosive acid bites deep into your flesh: lose 5 ENDURANCE points.

Only your innate Magnakai skill of Nexus saves you from sustaining what, for any lesser mortal, would have undoubtedly been a fatal injury. Shaken by this ferocious and unexpected attack, you scramble to the safety of a nearby pillar. Another stream of acid comes arching towards you, but only to splash harmlessly against the blue-green stone.

A glance around the pillar prompts a third stream of acid, only this time the creature ejects barely a trickle from its hook-like beak. It has exhausted its corrosive venom. Hungry for vengeance you emerge from your hiding place and face the octopoid once more, determined more than ever to defeat it in combat.

If you have a Bow and wish to use it, turn to **209**.
If you do not, turn to **164**.

224

Your weapon slams into the centre of the crystal and cracks it open. There is a flash of sparks, then the shimmering wall of light which imprisons Banedon flickers, and disappears completely.

Turn to **161**.

225

As you deal your final killing blow, the bodies of the three Vordaks rapidly dissolve into a foul-smelling green gas which is carried away on the breeze. Mindful that the combat may have attracted others of their kind, you sheathe your weapon and escape from the area as quickly as you can. At the end of the street you see an avenue leading off to the south, and another, blocked by rubble, heading off to the west.

If you wish to follow the avenue southwards, turn to **123**.
If you choose to clamber over the rubble which fills the entrance to the west avenue, turn to **31**.

226

As the last egorgh crashes lifelessly to the ground, you turn and hurry towards the adjoining passage. Sheathing your weapon as you run, you follow the passage for several minutes before arriving at an empty circular room. The only feature here is a rusty iron ladder fixed precariously to the wall, which ascends through a hole in the ceiling to a level above. There is no other exit from this chamber and so, with caution guiding your every move, you climb the rust-eaten rungs.

You rise through the hole to find yourself in a corridor which is strewn with human bones. Skeletons lie mixed in tangled heaps and many of the skulls and loose bones seem to have been gnawed. The psychic residues of pain and terror left by these luckless victims presses in upon your senses, making you feel queasy and claustrophobic. With pounding heart you advance along the bone-choked passage, stepping carefully through the skeletons to avoid making a sound. But you have taken less than a dozen steps when something unexpected makes you freeze in your tracks.

Turn to **186**.

227

Hastily you push Banedon aside then dive to avoid the falling net, the sheer speed with which you react saving you both from becoming trapped like two foxes in a snare. Quickly you spring to your feet and rush to help your fallen companion. As you stoop to lift him, you hear a deep voice cursing you quietly in the shadows. You turn to face the voice, weapon in hand, ready to cut him down. But you are shocked to the core when you see who it is who emerges into the grey light of the pen.

Turn to **47**.

228—*Illustration XI (opposite)*

Hurriedly you retreat, drawing a hand weapon in your defence as the two evil-eyed horrors come rushing forwards with murderous intent.

2 Xaghash: COMBAT SKILL 52   ENDURANCE 60

If you possess the Sommerswerd, double all bonuses it bestows upon you (for the duration of this combat only).

If you win the combat, turn to **239**.

229

A ghostly mist issues from the parting jaws of the throne-statue. You step back, your weapon raised, but it does nothing to protect you from the piercing screech which suddenly fills your head. You reel under the onslaught as, desperately, your Magnakai senses try to block this violent psychic attack. Before you can muster your defences to repel the attack, you suffer shock and injury to your central nervous system: lose 4 ENDURANCE points.

Turn to **253**.

230

Although you race along the street with the Death Knights hot on your heels, you are confident that you will soon out-run them. However, your confidence is severely shaken when you see that the way ahead is blocked by a hill of rubble, the remains of a collapsed watchtower.

If you possess the Discipline of Grand Huntmastery, and have reached the rank of Kai Grand Guardian, turn to **19**.

If you do not possess this skill, or have yet to reach this level of Kai Grand Mastery, turn to **199**.

XI. Two evil-eyed horrors rush forward with murderous intent.

231

With trepidation you follow the passage, praying all the while that Banedon's vision proves to be correct. Then at last your prayers are answered when, in the distance, you catch your first glimpse of the Zlanbeast pens.

You soon arrive at the entrance to the pens, where, from the safety of the shadows, you stop to observe the activity taking place inside. Lining the walls of the chamber you count more than a dozen cages, each holding a Zlanbeast or several smaller Kraan. Most are feeding, but there are some saddled ready for flight. One of these saddled Zlanbeast is perched nearby on a landing platform from where it casts its idle gaze upon the city far below.

You are contemplating how long it will take you and Banedon to reach the platform and climb aboard the waiting Zlanbeast, when suddenly you notice something strange that arouses your suspicions: there are no handlers or guards on duty in the pen.

If you possess Grand Pathsmanship, turn to **254**.
If you do not possess this skill, turn to **144**.

232

You pull the door slightly ajar then quickly gather up some sacks and boxes which you stack in a heap near the opening. The guttering wall torch that illuminates this chamber provides the flame to set this little makeshift bonfire alight. Soon the tinder-dry pile is ablaze, sending clouds of acrid blue-grey smoke billowing along the corridor towards the guards.

Pick a number from the *Random Number Table*.

If the number you have picked is 0–4, turn to **299**.
If it is 5–9, turn to **150**.

233

Barbed arrows whistle past you to shatter on the marble steps as you force your aching legs to cover the final twenty feet which separate you from the safety of the tunnel ahead.

Pick a number from the *Random Number Table*. If you possess Grand Pathsmanship, add 3 to the number you have picked.

If your total is *0–1*, turn to **62**.
If it is *2–6*, turn to **203**.
If it is *7* or more, turn to **273**.

234

You watch with fascination as the two wispy figures glide to a halt before the door. Their dark bodies are amorphous and indistinct, as if some spell or charm was preventing you from focusing clearly upon their true forms. They whisper words in a sombre musical tone, and slowly the slab of steel recedes into the wall.

A sudden probe invades your mind; you have been detected psychically. The wispy creatures solidify into the shapes of two dragon-like creatures, each the size of a small horse and, as they turn to face you, the probe in your mind is transformed into a red-hot lance of pain.

If you possess the Discipline of Kai-screen, turn to **149**.
If you do not possess this skill, turn to **39**.

235

The passage runs in an uninterrupted straight line for several hundred yards before arriving at a great circular room constructed of granite blocks. Cold air falls from a dark opening overhead and dozens of ropes and pulleys extend from this shaft, hanging down to touch the flagstoned floor. A large square door, furnished with brass and iron studs, is situated to your left. Apart from the shaft it appears to be the only exit from this chamber.

If you possess a Brass Key, turn to **122**.
If you do not have this Backpack Item, turn to **221**.

236

Beyond the door you find a small chamber, its wood-panelled walls hung with bridles and saddlery. You push the door closed and hold your breath as the footfalls of the Drakkarim steadily grow louder. To your relief, they pass by the door and continue without slowing down. When you can detect no sounds in the passageway, you leave this tack room and hurry away.

Turn to **287**.

237

Using your Magnakai Discipline of Telegnosis, you induce a trance that allows your conscious mind to leave your physical body and float across the fiery moat towards Banedon's prone form. Telepathically you call to him, trying to awaken him to consciousness, but you are unable to make contact. Then unexpectedly, your psychic calls are answered by a blood-chilling scream.

Horror floods your mind when you realize that the person before you is not your friend Banedon—it is a Helghast. As the creature rises and its features twist and distort before your gaze, you cast an anxious glance back across the moat to the place where your physical body stands. Through the great door come two Drakkarim guards behind a slavering boar-like creature which is straining on its leash. With relish they release the beast and it bounds towards your inanimate body, its jaws snapping wildly. Fear blazes scarlet as you will your spirit towards your body, desperate to reunite before the boar-thing tears your flesh to shreds.

Pick a number from the *Random Number Table*. If your current ENDURANCE points score is 20 or more, add 1 to the number you have picked. If your ENDURANCE is 19 or less, deduct 1.

If your total score is now *3* or less, turn to **258**.
If it is *4* or more, turn to **106**.

238

An arrow strikes your friend in the side and silently he falls to his knees, his hands still clinging to you for support. You stoop to lift him, but suddenly there is a flash of light and a blinding pain fills your head. The pain soon passes, but it is replaced by a blackness which fills your vision. You feel yourself falling forwards into an infinite void, as if you had, in the middle of a moonless night, just stepped over the edge of a towering cliff. Reluctantly you surrender to the sensation for it is the last sensation you will ever feel.

Sadly, your life and your quest end here.

239

You step back from the slain bodies of these two deadly foes, and lean against a table for support until your strength returns. By chance, you notice a strange key lying there. It has been carved from a green metallic substance which radiates a dim, phosphorescent light.

If you wish to keep this Green Key, mark it on your *Action Chart* as a Special Item which you carry in your tunic pocket.

As soon as your strength returns, you leave this chamber and press on with your search for Guildmaster Banedon.

Turn to **116**.

240

You sprint across the empty street and crouch at the base of the tower wall. The brick surface is plastered with mouldering grey cement and, as you look up at the roof twenty feet above, you steel yourself for what could prove to be a difficult climb.

Pick a number from the *Random Number Table*. If you possess a Rope, add 1 to the number you have picked. If you possess the Discipline of Grand Huntmastery, add 2.

If your total score is now *3* or less, turn to **219**.
If it is *4–6*, turn to **169**.
If it is *7* or more, turn to **54**.

241

A few minutes later you see two Giaks coming down the corridor, both carrying wooden buckets filled with sand. Hesitantly they push open the door, tip the sand haphazardly over the smouldering remains of the fire, then turn and scurry away.

For a while there is a hubbub of activity in the hallway as the guards and the Giaks speculate at length about the cause of the fire. While you are waiting for things to calm down, you must eat a Meal or lose 3 ENDURANCE points (unless you possess Grand Huntmastery).

Your first plan having failed, you decide instead to exercise your Kai skills of persuasion, aided by the use of the discarded Drakkar uniform.

Turn to **61**.

242

Defiantly you face the Helghast, your weapon at your side. The creature looks upon you and sneers, revealing two sharp fangs which protrude from its lower jaw. It emits a chilling cackle, full of hatred and contempt, and its eyes blaze like two hot coals as it confidently quickens its gait. You take a breath and utter the word of power that you learned from your mentor, Lord Rimoah: *"Gloar!"*

The word forms a ball of energy that speeds across the hall and slams into the approaching Helghast. The force of this power-word lifts the creature into the air and sends it tumbling, like some hideous rag doll, backwards into the flame-filled moat.

Open-mouthed, the two Drakkarim stumble to a halt and stare down into the all-consuming fire. Nervously they glance at each other, fearful of suffering a similar fate, but years of fierce battle discipline soon override their anxiety and, like two automatons, they raise their swords and continue to advance towards you.

Drakkarim veterans:
COMBAT SKILL 30   ENDURANCE 35

If you win this combat, turn to **293**.

243 —*Illustration XII (overleaf)*

The hovering shadow is changing shape once more. It expands and thickens, its misty outline now becoming hard and clearly defined. Your heart quickens when the transformation is complete for now you see before you a scaly dragon, with frosty-white skin and eyes as black as deep space. It fixes you with a murderous gaze and opens a mouth that is packed with razor-sharp fangs. Then a chilling gust of super-cold breath blows over you, leaving you shivering. Your Magnakai skills save you from being instantly frozen to death by this icy blast, but they will not keep you safe from the creature's fangs, its horny tail, or its sword-like claws. With a hungry growl, the dragon comes stalking forwards. Its jaw hangs open in expectation of an easy feast.

XII. *A scaly dragon with frosty white skin and razor-sharp fangs fixes you with a murderous gaze.*

Ice dragon (polymorphed Nadziranim):
COMBAT SKILL 48   ENDURANCE 52

If you win this combat, turn to **43**.

244

The Kraan glides towards the semi-ovoid platform and you swing one leg over its neck in readiness to leap from the saddle the moment it lands. With graceful agility, you jump the last few feet on to the platform and run through the open entrance. A Giak Kraan-handler suddenly appears before you, but your quick wits and Kai camouflage skills keep you from being seen. As he shuffles out on to the platform to tend to the screeching Kraan, you run towards the rear of the pen where there are two exits: one to the south, the other to the west.

If you wish to enter the south arch, turn to **154**.
If you choose to enter the west arch, turn to **48**.

245

An arrow clips your forearm, making you cry out in pained surprise: lose 3 ENDURANCE points.

"It's no good, Banedon," you shout, as you watch the Drakkarim rushing towards you, "we'll have to take our chances in the pen."

Cursing your predicament you turn around and hurry back towards the waiting ambush. But you have taken less than five steps inside the pen when an unexpected sound makes you look up. To your horror, you see a weighted net falling from the ceiling directly on to your heads.

Pick a number from the *Random Number Table*. If you have Grand Huntmastery, and have reached the rank of Kai Grand Guardian, add 3 to the number you have picked.

If your total is now *0–4*, turn to **23**.
If it is *5* or more, turn to **227**.

246

Before you land the killing blow which parts the head of this ghastly Vordak, it shrieks a cry of alarm that attracts a Zlanbeast circling in the smoky sky above. The winged reptilian answers its call by swooping down and raking you with its serrated beak.

Pick a number from the *Random Number Table* and add 1 to this number. The resulting total is equivalent to the number of ENDURANCE points you lose due to the Zlanbeast's attack.

Before you can retaliate, the winged creature soars into the air and disappears. Cursing its departure, you look down to see that the body of the slain Vordak is no longer there. It has transformed into a foul-smelling green gas.

Mindful that the Zlanbeast might summon others of its kind, you sheathe your weapon and escape from the area as quickly as you can. At the end of the street you see an avenue leading off to the south, and another, blocked by rubble, heading off to the west.

If you wish to follow the avenue southwards, turn to **123**.
If you choose to clamber over the rubble which fills the entrance to the west avenue, turn to **31**.

247

Carefully you step over the twitching remains of the three Plaak and continue along the tunnel without looking back. Several hundred yards later you arrive at an empty circular room. The only feature here is a rusty iron ladder fixed precariously to the wall, which ascends through a hole in the ceiling to a level above. There is no other exit from this chamber and so, with caution guiding your every move, you climb the rust-eaten rungs.

You rise through the hole to find yourself in a corridor which is strewn with human bones. Skeletons lie mixed in tangled heaps and many of the skulls and loose bones seem to have been gnawed. The psychic residues of pain and terror left by these luckless victims presses in upon your senses, making you feel queasy and claustrophobic. With pounding heart you advance along the bone-choked passage, stepping carefully through the skeletons to avoid making a sound. But you have taken less than a dozen steps when something unexpected makes you freeze in your tracks.

Turn to **186**.

248

You feel the heat singe your skin as the stream of flame comes speeding towards your face. Guided purely by instinct, you throw yourself to the floor in a desperate attempt to avoid being sprayed by this stream of liquid fire.

Pick a number from the *Random Number Table*. If you possess Grand Huntmastery, add 3 to the number you have picked.

If your total score is now 6 or less, turn to **89**.
If it is 7 or more, turn to **279**.

249

The vines are rope-thick and immensely tough. Despite their thorns, which repeatedly snag your cloak, you find it easy to climb up the shaft to the level above. However, as you approach the level, the thorns begin to grow at an alarming rate. They pierce your clothing and, when they puncture your skin, you feel an agonising pain course through your body. Like the teeth of a vampire, the thorns allow the bloodsucking vines to leech your life's blood: lose 10 EN-DURANCE points.

Half-blinded by the pain and loss of blood, you fail to see the pair of Drakkarim Death Knights who are standing close to the edge of the shaft on this level. Your cries of agony startle them and, with brutal efficiency, they tear you away from your thorny prison and throw you to the ground. Through a red haze of pain you glimpse them unsheathing their swords with the intention of striking you dead.

Drakkarim Death Knights:
COMBAT SKILL 42   ENDURANCE 37

If you win this combat, turn to **197**.

250

In desperation you throw up your hands to shield your face as the spiked log comes hurtling down the stairs. It hits you, impaling your chest upon two of its deadly sharpened staves, and rolls you down the stairs to the street below. You suffer terrible wounds and, mercifully, death is instantaneous.

Tragically, your life and your quest end here in Kaag.

251

The passage leads directly to a huge hall constructed of fiery red granite. It is lit by scores of braziers placed at regular intervals around the walls, and the atmosphere is heavy with the stench of ash and sulphur. Tapestries woven of metal thread adorn the far wall, making it gleam dully in the scarlet light. They depict scenes of evil grandeur: vast molten landscapes, like the surfaces of suns, all furiously ablaze.

Cautiously you step into the hall, passing between two great pillars which flank the entrance. The air is scorchingly hot (although you have experienced hotter places here in Kaag) and your senses are dulled by it. Far off in the distance, through the rising heat, you glimpse a tunnel which descends to a lower level of the citadel.

You are contemplating avoiding this hall by turning back and retracing your steps to the junction, when suddenly you hear the sound of flapping wings high above. You look up and a shiver runs the length of your spine when you see two malicious eyes staring down at you from the shadows of the roof.

If you possess Kai-screen, turn to **18**.
If you do not possess mastery of this Discipline, turn to **163**.

252

You feel your strength waning as the Helghast's steely fingers claw relentlessly into your throat: lose 4 ENDURANCE points. In sheer desperation you twist and writhe like a snake in a last-ditch attempt to free yourself from its deadly grip. For an instant its hold falters and you exploit this weakness to the full. You grab the creature's sleeves and, with a swerve of your hips, you send it hurtling over your shoulder. With a wail of abject terror, the Helghast is sent tumbling off the bridge to fall, face first, into the flame-filled moat.

Open-mouthed, the two Drakkarim stumble to a halt and stare down into the moat. Nervously they glance at each other, fearful of suffering a similar fate, then they turn and run towards the open chamber door. Determined not to let them escape, you give chase and catch up with them within a few yards of the entrance.

Drakkarim: COMBAT SKILL 26   ENDURANCE 35

If you win this combat, turn to **293**.

253

From out of the mist-filled jaw there emerges a small black creature covered in shaggy fur. Its head is white, cut with dark bony ridges and studded with running sores that encircle its flaming red eyes.

You raise your weapon and get ready to strike as it stalks nearer, but your concentration is momentarily broken when you notice a wispy shadow emerging from the alcove on the far side of the hall. It is a Nadziranim sorcerer. Fearful of its purpose, you turn away from the furry creature and make a dash towards the ivory staircase, intent on reaching Banedon as quickly as possible. The stalking creature, thinking that you are running in fear, immediately gives chase and comes bounding towards you, determined to intercept you before you reach the steps.

If you have a Bow and wish to use it, turn to **40**.
If you do not, turn to **148**.

254

You bring your advanced tracking senses to bear and, almost at once, you detect an ambush has been laid for you in this pen. An elaborate magical screen has been erected to camouflage and keep hidden the warriors who are, at this very moment, lying in wait for you and Banedon to appear.

Anxiously you peer into the pen, scrutinizing every shadow for some clue to the ambusher's whereabouts, but you are unable to spot their positions. The saddled Zlanbeast looks so inviting, yet your hopes of escape are tempered by the desire to keep yourself and Guildmaster Banedon alive.

If you wish to attempt to reach the Zlanbeast and escape as quickly as you can, hopefully before the ambushers can stop you, turn to **82**.
If you decide to retreat from the pens and go in search of an alternative escape route, turn to **128**.

255

As the Doomwolf howls its death cry and crashes to the floor, you hear the sound of booted feet running along the passageway outside. The noise of combat and the Doomwolf's last howl have drawn a squad of Drakkarim to this cell.

Quickly you cross to the room's solitary window. It is criss-crossed with iron bars, but on closer examination you discover that they are loose and badly corroded. A swift blow with the heels of your hands is enough to dislodge them, allowing you to escape with ease.

Outside the window there is a covered courtyard. You crouch in the shadows while you wait for a group of Drakkarim stablehands to disappear, then you cross to the far side, climb a low wall, and make your escape into the ruins beyond.

For over a mile you wend your way through derelict buildings before you happen upon an avenue which is surprisingly clear of debris and obstructions. You are conscious that perhaps it is too clear, offering you no cover at all from the tall buildings that line this route to the centre of Kaag. You decide to trust to the ruins rather than run the risk of being detected out in the open. However, within a matter of minutes you are confronted by a new hazard. The ground in this section of the city is unsafe. It is riddled with potholes and concealed cellars, covered by rotten wooden beams and slabs of paper-thin plaster. Suddenly one such section gives way beneath your feet and you find yourself falling headlong into coal-black darkness.

Pick a number from the *Random Number Table*. If you have the Discipline of Grand Huntmastery, add 2 to the number you have picked.

If your total score is now *0–5*, turn to **28**.
If it is *6* or more, turn to **44**.

256

Your spell causes the sphere to vibrate uncontrollably. Tiny cracks appear in its crystal surface then, with a flash of sparks, it breaks in two. At once the shimmering wall of light which imprisons Banedon flickers, then disappears completely.

Turn to **161**.

257

Unable to progress any further in this direction, you return to the Kraan pen and enter the west arch. There you discover a flight of stairs which ascends through several levels of the citadel until it finally emerges in a vast hall. This chilly place is festooned with icy stalagtites. In the dim distance you see the yellowy glow of a warmer chamber and you hurry towards it, taking care not to slip on the treacherous, frost-covered floor.

You are near the centre of this chamber when the temperature drops dramatically. Unless you possess the Discipline of Grand Nexus, you lose 5 ENDURANCE points due to the extreme cold.

To continue, turn to **116**.

258

You rejoin your physical body barely seconds before the creature attacks, but the shock of such a swift transition leaves you temporarily paralysed and unable to move: lose 3 ENDURANCE points.

As the numbness fades, the boar-thing slams into your chest and sends you reeling backwards across the glassy floor towards the moat. Its great curved tusks deeply gouge your arm and shoulder (lose a further 5 ENDURANCE points). Unsteadily you rise to your feet and draw your weapon as the beast attacks once more, this time with its head down, in an attempt to butt you into the fiery moat.

Gnagusk: COMBAT SKILL 41   ENDURANCE 45

If you win this combat, turn to **281**.

259 —*Illustration XIII (overleaf)*

You increase your speed as you approach the iron door and get ready to push against it, expecting great resistance but, to your complete surprise, the heavy portal swings open the instant you reach out to touch it. A gust of cooling air wafts in your face, encouraging you to step into the hall which lies beyond. Swiftly the iron door slams shut behind you but you pay it no heed. The refreshing coolness and the awesome spectacle of the hall itself commands your complete attention.

Tiers of glittering gold-veined marble descend to a circular hall where a ring of fluted copper pillars support a platform, shaped like the foredeck of some great ship. Multicoloured rays stream from a crystal sphere suspended above this platform, creating a cage of flickering light at its centre. Sitting in this radiant cage is a pale-skinned man with long blond hair. His knees are drawn up to his chin and his eyes are closed, as if asleep. You recognize him to be Banedon, but still mindful of your encounter with the Helghast, you reserve your judgement.

A narrow staircase, its handrails carved and fashioned from the tusks of Kalte mammoths, leads directly to the platform. Cautiously you descend the tiers, cross the floor, and advance towards these stairs, stopping only when you reach a granite throne positioned directly opposite the staircase. The back and arms of this crude seat have been chiselled to resemble a lion-like creature sitting on its haunches, and it is from here that you attempt to communicate telepathically with the sleeping man.

At first there is no response. Then, wearily, he raises his head and forces open his eyes. His face is haggard and lined

XIII. *Multicoloured rays stream from a crystal sphere into the circular hall where the blond, pale-skinned man sits.*

with fatigue, but the look of extreme tiredness slowly changes to a smile of recognition when he sees you.

"Lone Wolf..." the words form slowly in your mind, *"thank Ishir you've found me ..."*

Convinced now that he truly is your friend Banedon, you rush towards the steps, eager to free him from his prison. Then you sense something is wrong and you skid to a halt at the foot of the steps. Banedon's weary smile has changed to a wide-eyed look of fear.

Turn to **207**.

260

The moment you set foot upon the dusty floor you discover that it is not what it seems. It is not solid and rapidly you sink up to your chest in a pool of fine grey grit. You throw out your arms to try to slow your descent, but the more you struggle to get free, the faster you sink.

If you possess the Discipline of Kai-alchemy, turn to **142**.

If you do not possess this skill or do not wish to use it, turn to **205**.

261

Eventually your persistence pays off. The lock clicks open and the door swings back to allow you to pass through into the chamber beyond.

Turn to **283**.

262

Fifty yards on, the passage turns sharply to the left and you find yourself staring at an iron-banded door. Luckily this portal is unlocked and you hurry through it, pausing only for a few seconds to bolt it shut behind you before continuing on your way.

Shortly you arrive at a deserted stairwell where you begin a long and laborious ascent. You climb more than sixty levels of the citadel before reaching the top. During your climb, unless you possess the Discipline of Grand Huntmastery, you must eat a Meal or lose 3 ENDURANCE points.

Directly opposite the landing at the top of the stairs is a massive bronze portal, its surface inlaid with intricate symbols cast in silver and gleaming gold. A sleeping Drakkar sentry is seated beside this huge door. He snores softly, his leather-helmeted head tilted to his shoulder and his spear lying uselessly at his feet. He is oblivious to your presence as you glide past him and silently push open the great door.

Beyond the portal lies a massive circular hall, its walls lined with slabs of smooth black rock. Its domed ceiling rises more than a hundred feet to point directly above a dais positioned at the centre of the chamber. A flame-filled moat surrounds this circular platform whereupon lies the unconscious body of a blond-haired man clad in silken blue robes. Your spirits soar when you recognize the designs embroidered upon the robe for they are the symbols of the Brotherhood of the Crystal Star—the magician's guild of Sommerlund. For a moment your joy at having found your friend is dampened when your Magnakai senses warn that great danger is close at hand. Prompted by this presentiment you hurry towards the moat, to where an iron drawbridge stands raised, and begin to crank its handle in order to lower it across the fiery divide.

If you possess the Discipline of Kai-alchemy, and wish to use it, turn to **16**.

If you possess Telegnosis and wish to use it, turn to **237**.

If you possess neither of these Grand Master Disciplines, or choose not to use them, turn to **127**.

263

The creature tries to dodge your speeding shaft but it is too slow. The arrow skewers its lower jaw, causing the beast to shriek out loudly in pained surprise. However, despite this fearful wounding, it does not break off its attack. With chilling disregard for pain, it wrenches the arrow from its jaw and hurls it aside. Unnerved by this display of bravado, you shoulder your bow as, with a gurgling shriek, the beast comes bounding forwards. You get ready to meet its advance yet, when it is but ten feet away, it suddenly opens its bloodstained mouth wide and spews forth a stream of white-hot liquid fire.

If you possess the Discipline of Grand Nexus, turn to **288**.

If you do not possess this Grand Master Discipline, turn to **248**.

264

You struggle to remove the precious herb from your Backpack. Then, with great difficulty, you force yourself to swallow the dry, golden leaves.

Within a few minutes you feel the Oede countering the insidious virus. Your temperature drops and very soon the battle is over; the virus has been totally eradicated from your bloodstream.

Once you have fully recovered, you check your equipment before climbing the steps which lead out of this grim cellar.

Turn to **147**.

265

You utter a power-word which you direct at the creature's head. The concussive force of this spell hits the beast full in its face, making it falter and stagger back. But it does not delay its advance for very long. Its sheer size and strength enables it to withstand the blow and continue its advance, now doubly determined to fulfil Cadak's command. Hastily you draw a hand weapon as the shadow of the angry beast falls upon you.

Turn to **111**.

266

You climb the stairs and emerge in the centre of a hall on the level above. This vault-like room contains a wealth of grim exhibits, hung upon the walls and displayed in glass-fronted cases. The skulls of rare creatures are displayed beside tanned hides and jewel-encrusted bones. One item in particular catches your eye: it is a statuette, fashioned in the likeness of Darklord Zagarna.

If you wish to keep this Statuette of Zagarna, mark it on your *Action Chart* as a Special Item which you keep in your Backpack. If you already carry your maximum quota, you must discard one item in its favour.

To continue, turn to **178**.

267

You lower your head and force yourself to trudge uphill against the storm, your feet sinking ankle-deep into the barren volcanic dust with every laboured step. Keeping your eyes shut tight against the stinging, gritty winds, you trust solely to your Magnakai senses to steer you on the correct course towards the Darkland city. Only when you reach the top of the ridge do you attempt to look around at the bleak domain. The *Skyrider* is lost from sight, shrouded by the swirling grey clouds. Kaag, too, remains hidden for some minutes until a sudden lull in the storm clears the southern vista. Then, what you see makes your blood run cold.

In your lifetime you have gazed upon many awe-inspiring cities, but few compare with the enormous size and monstrous grandeur of Kaag. A coal-black curtain-wall constructed of massive blocks of smooth, featureless stone, encircles this city, forty miles wide. At its centre there arises a gigantic citadel of black marble, pyramid-shaped and slitted with numerous vents to allow what passes for air to circulate within. Its highest point towers two miles above the desolate plain. Thunder booms and streaks of blue-white lightning earth themselves against its walls, drawn from the rolling storm clouds gathered menacingly overhead.

At first the fortress seems wholly impregnable, then you notice that the outer wall is not entirely intact. Illuminated by the infrequent electrical flashes, you see that a mile-long section of the eastern battlements has fallen outwards to litter the plain with huge black cubes of stone. You are surprised to note that no attempt has been made to repair this breach and, consequently, access to the city can be effected here with relative ease.

Turn to **202**.

268

Holding Banedon firmly in place across your shoulders, you climb the tiered steps towards the tunnel. The cold dark passage looks most uninviting, but when you hear the sound of a patrol approaching the main doors, you forget your reticence and hurry along the passage to avoid them.

The dingy passage descends by slope and stair to a rectangular hall which is lined with ancient stone statues, their features made unrecognizable by age. Tar-soaked torches fixed to the two longest walls illuminate this musty chamber with a flickering amber light, and the air is heavy with their oily stench. In the distance you see an archway and the passage continuing away into darkness.

If you wish to stop here for a few minutes and try to revive Banedon, turn to **25**.

If you decide to press on without stopping here, turn to **151**.

269

The fell creature pins you to the ground and its steely hands tighten like two vices around your throat. Blackness invades the edges of your vision and, although you twist and buck to break free, you feel your strength ebbing away fast. Soon you are too weak to struggle any longer and, reluctantly, you slip away into a sleep from which you will never awaken.

Sadly, your life and your quest end here.

270

You propel yourself out of the ruins and sprint across the street towards the tower stairs. Everything seems to be going to plan until you are halfway up, when suddenly there is a loud *clunk*. You look up and, to your horror, you see a heavy wooden log, pierced by a criss-cross of metal staves sharpened at either end, come crashing down the steps towards you. The brutal face of a Drakkar peers over the edge of the tower parapet, watching with gleeful expectation as the great spiked log bounces on the steps and comes spinning straight at you.

Pick a number from the *Random Number Table*. If you possess the Discipline of Grand Huntmastery, add 2 to the number you have picked.

If your total score is now *3* or less, turn to **250**.
If it is *4–7*, turn to **36**.
If it is *8* or more, turn to **300**.

271

You have taken less than a dozen steps along the tunnel when the soles of your boots begin to smoulder and give off wisps of smoke.

If you possess the Discipline of Grand Nexus, turn to **33**. If you do not possess mastery of this Discipline, turn to **96**.

272

Using the Brotherhood spell of "*Mind Charm*," reinforced by your powerful psychic ability, you convince the two guards to allow you to pass unhindered. They draw back their spears and at once the crackling crimson energy which united them ceases to arc between the shafts.

"You may enter," they say, without any trace of emotion, and as they stand aside, so the two great doors glide silently open. Steeling yourself, you stride towards the blazing purple light which fills the chamber.

Turn to **159**.

273

The sound of arrows whistling towards your back provides all the incentive you need to keep running. You bound up the steps and, as the deadly barbed shafts fly past only inches from your back and legs, you carry your friend headlong into the tunnel.

The dingy passage beyond descends by slope and stair to a rectangular hall which is lined with ancient stone statues, their features made unrecognizable by age. Tar-soaked torches fixed to the two longest walls illuminate this musty chamber with a flickering amber light, and the air is heavy with their oily stench. In the distance you see an archway and the passage continuing away into darkness. You are breathless from your narrow escape and feel the need to rest.

If you wish to stop here for a few minutes to rest, turn to **25.**

If you decide to press on without stopping here, turn to **151.**

274

Desperately you call upon your psychic defences to shield your mind from this attack, but your reflexes have been dulled by the fatigue of recent combat and you react too slowly to prevent some of the Vordaks' destructive energy from reaching your psyche. Lose 4 ENDURANCE points.

Turn to **187.**

275

You call upon your Magnakai discipline of Animal Control in an attempt to halt the egorgh advance, but your powers of persuasion are not strong enough to turn away all three of these fearsome hulks. For a moment they halt and settle on their haunches, then, with a chorus of frantic screeches, the creatures come leaping towards you, their mouths agape and their claws extended ready for the kill.

3 Egorghs: COMBAT SKILL 37   ENDURANCE 42

These creatures are particularly susceptible to psychic attacks; double all bonuses you would normally be entitled to if you choose to employ psychic attacks during this combat.

If you win the combat, turn to **226.**

276

With trepidation you step into the glimmering column of light and immediately you feel yourself begin to rise. Bands of darkness flick past with growing rapidity, each one a passing floor level of this mountainous citadel. Then you feel yourself slowing to a halt. The column fades and you find yourself standing on a metal dais in the centre of a domed chamber. Ahead you see a great door, forged of Kagonite, and beside it there is a narrow staircase leading down.

As you approach the door, you notice the lock that secures it. It is inlaid with a series of numbers and, at once, you recognize that they are component parts of a combination lock. One number in the sequence is missing. By tapping the correct number upon the blank square, you will cause the lock to disengage.

Study the following sequence of numbers carefully. When you think you know what the missing number is, turn to the page that is identical to your answer.

If you guess incorrectly, or if you cannot answer the puzzle, turn instead to **38**.

277

The bolt of lightning hits the sphere and causes it to vibrate, but the bolt itself is not strong enough to shatter or dislodge it. The curtain of light imprisoning Banedon remains intact and you are forced to abandon the spell and try some other way of freeing him.

If you possess a Bow and wish to use it, turn to **211**.
If you possess Magi-magic, and have reached the rank of Kai Grand Guardian, turn to **94**.
If you do not have a Bow, do not possess the Discipline of Magi-magic, or have yet to reach the required Kai rank, turn instead to **292**.

278

As the last of the Drakkarim falls dead at your feet, you turn and help Banedon who has been wounded during the fight. He is bleeding from the upper right arm, but when you examine the wound you discover that it is not as deep as you had first feared. You are helping him to stand when you hear a man's voice cursing you quietly in the shadows. You turn to face this voice, weapon in hand, ready to attack. You command him to show himself, but you are shocked to the core when you see who it is who emerges into the grey light of the pen.

Turn to **47**.

279

Your lightning-fast reflexes save you from being hit by the searing stream of liquid fire. Several droplets splash your tunic and it catches alight (lose 1 ENDURANCE point), but you quickly extinguish the flames. Coolly you raise your weapon and stare the creature defiantly in the eye as it gets ready to pounce.

Turn to **34**.

280

Calling upon the secrets of your new-found Kai mastery, you summon from the ground a dense mist which rapidly fills the space between you and the advancing Death Knights. The instant they are lost to sight, you throw yourself flat on your chest to avoid their volley of deadly bolts. They fire, but their missiles pass over where you lie and shatter harmlessly against a distant wall.

Before they can retreat from the mist to reload, you spring to your feet and rush forwards, catching them unaware. You dodge through their line with ease, and by the time they realize that you have evaded them, and start to give chase, you have passed the junction and have begun to run along the street opposite.

Turn to **230**.

281

As you pull away from the body of the dead Gnagusk, the iron drawbridge comes crashing down. The sudden noise makes you spin around and you see the Helghast as it comes rushing across the flaming moat. As it runs, its skin darkens and peels away in tatters as if it was being scorched by some invisible fire. The Drakkarim meet the creature at the end of the bridge and, together, they turn and advance upon you.

If you possess Kai-alchemy, and wish to use it, turn to **5**.
If you possess Magi-magic, and wish to use it, turn to **242**.
If you possess Kai-surge, and wish to use it, turn to **115**.
If you have none of these Grand Master Disciplines, or choose not to use any of them, turn instead to **41**.

282

You invoke the words of the Brotherhood spell *"Mind Charm"* and direct it at the sleeping Drakkar. Telepathically, you ask him where the Sommlending wizard is being held prisoner, and at first you detect no reply. You ask again, and this time you get a faint response.

"Above . . . high above . . . in old Zagarna's courtroom."

Satisfied that you have gleaned all the information you are likely to from this Drakkar, you climb the stairs and emerge in the centre of a hall on the level above. This vault-like room contains a wealth of grim exhibits, hung upon the walls or displayed in glass-fronted cases. The skulls of rare creatures are displayed beside tanned hides and jewel-encrusted bones. One item in particular catches your eye: it is a statuette, fashioned in the likeness of Darklord Zagarna.

If you wish to keep this Statuette of Zagarna, mark it on your *Action Chart* as a Special Item which you keep in your Backpack. If you already carry your maximum quota, you must discard one item in its favour.

To continue, turn to **178**.

283

Beyond the door awaits a sumptuous chamber dominated by a magnificent fireplace crafted from blocks of glassy rock. The walls are hung with fine tapestries, looted from the Stornlands during times of war, and you note that the furniture is carved from best Durenese oak.

You pass through the chamber into an adjoining passage which leads to a library. As you enter, you disturb a robed creature seated at a lectern. Before it can rise or raise the alarm, you draw your weapon and silence it with a swift blow to the base of its skull. Pulling back its hood reveals it to be a Liganim, a thrall of the Nadziranim sorcerers.

Suddenly you hear movement and glance up to see another liganim peering over the parapet of a gallery which encircles the upper level of this library. The creature, having witnessed the slaying of its companion, lets out a horrified squeal and turns to run towards an archway on the far side of the gallery. Determined to prevent his escape, you lower Banedon to the floor then rush towards a flight of wooden stairs that also lead to the archway. However, as you near the landing at the top of these stairs, two more of the creatures appear from either side, with wands gripped in their clawed hands. They shout a spell-word in the dark tongue and a crackling curtain of energy flares between the two rods, blocking your path. The power-wall looks formidable, but you sense at once that it is really quite weak.

If you possess Kai-alchemy, and wish to use it, turn to **117**.
If you wish to run straight through this magical barrier, turn to **208**.
If you choose to retreat down the stairs and rejoin your unconscious companion, turn to **13**.

284

Outside the window there is a covered courtyard. You crouch in the shadows while you wait for a group of Drakkarim stablehands to finish their duties here, then you cross to the far side, climb over a low wall, and make your escape into the ruins beyond.

For over a mile you wend your way through derelict buildings before you happen upon an avenue which is surprisingly clear of debris and obstructions. You are conscious that perhaps it is too clear, offering you no cover at all from the tall buildings that line this route to the centre of Kaag.

You decide to trust to the ruins rather than run the risk of being detected out in the open. However, within a matter of minutes you are confronted by a new hazard. The ground in this section of the city is unsafe. It is riddled with potholes and concealed cellars, covered by rotten wooden beams and slabs of paper-thin plaster. Suddenly one such section gives way beneath your feet and you find yourself falling headlong into coal-black darkness.

Pick a number from the *Random Number Table*. If you have the Discipline of Grand Huntmastery, add 2 to the number you have picked.

If your score is now *0–5*, turn to **28**.
If it is *6* or more, turn to **44**.

285

As you raise your enchanted weapon, the Helghast shrieks in alarm as it recognizes the power you wield. Immediately it breaks off its advance and staggers back towards the bridge, desperate to flee its nemesis. Determinedly you chase after this evil being and, as it reaches the drawbridge, you come to within a sword's length of its skull.

"Die, foul spawn!" you cry, and with one fell sweep of your arm, you send the creature tumbling from the bridge to be consumed by the hungry flames below. Open-mouthed, the two Drakkarim stumble to a halt and stare down into the moat. Nervously they glance at each other, fearful of suffering a similar fate, then they turn and run towards the open door. Determined not to let them escape, you give chase and catch up with them within a few yards of the entrance.

Drakkarim: COMBAT SKILL 26   ENDURANCE 35

If you win this combat, turn to **293**.

286

You leave the chamber by means of a passageway that leads to a circular hall. Here, a column of shimmering blue light descends from a hole in the middle of the roof and passes through a similar hole in the floor. Your senses tingle as you gaze at this column, for you immediately recognize its purpose. Within the confines of the light, gravity is greatly reduced. It is used as a means of transportation, an elevator that can take you to other levels of Kaag, either above or below. The last time you saw one of these devices was in Helgedad, the former principal stronghold of the Darklands.

If you wish to step into the transporter beam, turn to **276**.
If you choose to ignore it, you can leave the chamber by

means of a spiral staircase adjacent to its north wall.
Turn to **100**.

287

The passage ends at an open door which leads to a covered
courtyard. You wait for a group of Drakkarim stablehands to
leave the yard, then you cross to the far side, climb over a
low wall, and make your way into the ruins beyond.

For over a mile you wend your way through derelict buildings before you happen upon an avenue which is surprisingly clear of debris and obstructions. You are conscious
that perhaps it is too clear, offering you no cover at all
from the tall buildings which line this route to the centre of
Kaag.

You decide to trust to the ruins rather than run the risk of
being detected out in the open. However, within a matter of
minutes you are confronted by a new hazard. The ground in
this section of the city is unsafe. It is riddled with potholes
and concealed cellars, covered by rotten wooden beams and
slabs of paper-thin plaster. Suddenly one such section gives
way beneath your feet and you find yourself falling headlong into coal-black darkness.

Pick a number from the *Random Number Table*. If you have
the Discipline of Grand Huntmastery, add 2 to the number
you have picked.

  If your total score is now *0–5*, turn to **28**.
  If it is *6* or more, turn to **44**.

288

Your lightning-fast reflexes and your mastery of the Discipline of Grand Nexus saved you from being hit by the
searing stream of liquid fire. Droplets splash on your tunic
and it catches alight, but you quickly extinguish the flames

before stepping forwards to engage the creature in mortal combat.

Turn to **168**.

289

Steadily you draw an arrow and take aim at the approaching beast. As the boar-thing comes bounding on to the draw-bridge, you let fly your shaft at a point between its great curved tusks.

Pick a number from the *Random Number Table*. If you possess the Discipline of Grand Weaponmastery with Bow, add 5 to the number you have picked.

If your total score is now *5* or less, turn to **88**.
If it is *6–11*, turn to **189**.
If it is *12* or more, turn to **30**.

290

Guided by instinct, you hurriedly retrieve the statuette from your Backpack and hold it high above your head. Instantly the flames subside and, as the terrible heat dissipates, you hear the voice boom out once more.

"Very well, loyal acolyte," it says, in an almost conde-scending tone, "you may pass."

With a hiss of escaping air, the solid, blue-green metal door slides open to reveal a dark tunnel leading away from the chamber. Eager to continue your search for your captive friend Banedon without further delay, you slip the statuette into your Backpack and hurry through the archway into the darkness beyond.

Turn to **171**.

291

The street continues beyond the mound, heading due south towards the great citadel, the shadow of this edifice looming ever larger. Soon the street opens out to a wide concourse which encircles the citadel and offers access to its great Northern Door. The entire door is made of black iron, streaked with rust. Turrets jut from either side, on top of which you can see giant cannon-like weapons, similar to those once employed by the Darklords aboard their ironclad fleets. From the cover of a ruined house you watch the traffic of Giaks and Drakkarim, all clad in orange uniforms bearing the mark of a bloodied scythe. The more you stare at the citadel, the more you are sure that this is where Banedon is being held prisoner. However, entry into the citadel itself looks to be impossible, until, that is, an opportunity unexpectedly presents itself.

Turn to **107**.

292

Using your weapon, you draw back your right hand and take aim at the sphere. For someone of your ability, it would be difficult to miss hitting this target with a thrown weapon. But will it strike with sufficient force to break or dislodge the sphere?

Pick a number from the *Random Number Table*. If you have Grand Huntmastery, add 3 to the number you have picked.

If your total score is 5 or less, turn to **84**.
If it is 6 or more, turn to **224**.

293

Breathless from combat, you step away from the two dead Drakkarim, sheathe your weapon, and wipe your blood-spattered brow with the back of your hand. Then, in order to leave no trace, you drag both of the corpses to the edge of the moat and consign them, and their weapons, to the hungry flames.

A narrow passage near the main door provides an exit from this hall. This leads into a wider tunnel which is flanked on both sides by cages, all empty but showing signs of having recently been occupied by war-dogs and the like. Beyond the cells you discover a chamber strewn with wooden boxes, trunks, sacks and several oak casks. It, too, is empty, although in the far wall there is a stout door with a spyhole drilled at its centre. Your keen Kai senses detect the faint sound of squealing coming from the other side of this door.

If you wish to search this chamber, turn to **99**.
If you wish to peek through the spyhole, turn to **192**.

294

You pull on the reins, hoping to steer the Zlanbeast higher in time to clear the whistling cloud of bolts, but the beast lacks the speed and strength to perform such an exacting manoeuvre.

Suddenly a starburst of pain erupts in your head and the taste of blood fills your mouth. You have been hit in the skull by one of the iron-tipped missiles and death is instantaneous.

Tragically, your life and your quest end here on the very threshold of victory.

295

Your efforts to escape are rewarded but only after immense exertion: lose 3 ENDURANCE points. You catch hold of the archway and pull yourself to safety, yet your submersion has cost you your money pouch and one item from your Backpack, lost when you first fell into the dusty pool. Erase all your Gold Crowns, and the first item recorded on your Backpack Items list.

As the effects of the spell wear off, you leave this sinister chamber and head off along the tunnel.

Turn to **71**.

296

Despite your hasty casting of the spell, your invisible shield protects you fully against the speeding crossbow bolts. The sight of you having survived such a rain of missiles leaves many of their number staring open-mouthed with shock. You seize the initiative and dodge through their line with ease, and by the time they realize that you have evaded them, and start to give chase, you have already passed the junction and begun to run along the street opposite.

Turn to **230**.

297

You take aim at the point mid-way between the creature's feral eyes, then release your straining bowstring.

Pick a number from the *Random Number Table*. If you possess Weaponmastery with Bow, add 5 to the number you have picked.

If your total score is 6 or less, turn to **15**.
If your total score is 7 or more, turn to **263**.

298

Quickly you transfer your bow to your left hand and raise your right, pointing it directly at the shimmering surface of the pool. The octopoid is within a few feet of the pool's edge when you shout out the power words that trigger the Brotherhood spell *"Lightning Hand."* Immediately, a brilliant flash of blue-white light engulfs your palm and a bolt of flame shoots from your index finger towards the pool.

Turn to **45**.

299

The guards see the approaching clouds of smoke and immediately raise the alarm. Aided by a passing group of Drakkarim and Giaks, the two silver-clad guardians come thundering along the corridor and skid to a halt outside the door. You hear them coughing and cursing, then the door flies open and two luckless Giaks are thrust into the smoky room with orders to put out the blaze.

Utilizing your Magnakai camouflage skills, and helped by the smoke and confusion, you manage to slip past the Giaks and the others and hurry along the corridor towards the distant doors. To your surprise, the two massive portals open as you approach them. A purple glare blinds you momentarily, forcing you to raise your hand to shield your eyes, but still you keep running until you have passed through the doors.

Turn to **159**.

300

In the face of this deadly trap you draw on all your skills and agility in order to save yourself from a grisly death. As the log falls upon you, you turn sideways and dive headlong between the spinning staves. You land heavily on the stone steps, bruising your hands (lost 1 ENDURANCE point), but you have successfully avoided being impaled upon the terrible steel spikes.

Turn to **182**.

301

You climb across the shattered masonry and take cover near an empty window which overlooks the square. Minutes later you see a thin figure clad in red robes, accompanied by six grime-smeared Giaks, enter the square from an alley on the far side. At once you recognize the skeletal features of the robed one: it is a Vordak, an undead spawn of the Darklords.

The Vordak raises a bony hand and immediately its companions halt. Then, with a sweep of its arm, it slowly scans the ruins bordering the square.

If you possess the Discipline of Kai-screen, and have reached the rank of Kai Grand Guardian, turn to **73**.

If you do not possess this skill, or have yet to reach this level of Grand Mastery, turn to **112**.

302—Illustration XIV (overleaf)

Below you is the South Gate of Kaag. Its surface is covered by the hide of Nyxator, preserved by the Darklords as a trophy of Naar's evil power. Nyxator was the first servant of the God Kai to appear on Magnamund and the form he chose to adopt was that of a great dragon. He was the first recipient of Kai's wisdom, a wisdom he encapsulated in the Lorestones for the future good of all who follow the way of Kai.

You stare down at the face of your ancient ancestor and, for a fleeting moment, you detect the trace of a smile upon its fossilized lips. Then, in the next instant, you plunge into a bank of stormy grey cloud and the dread city of Kaag is lost to view.

By the time you find your way back to the *Skyrider*, the storm has blown itself out. Your return is met with cheers and joyous celebration for your quest has been a great success. Lord Rimoah is especially pleased and he praises you warmly:

"Against all odds," he says, his voice filled with pride, "you have rescued our friend from the nightmare fortress of Kaag and delivered him safely into the arms of his loyal crew."

Congratulations. Grand Master Lone Wolf. You have triumphed once again, proving beyond doubt that you embody the ideals of the Kai. You have saved your closest friend from the clutches of the evil druid Cadak and confounded his plans.

Yet the fight against Evil goes ever on. Soon your courage and skills will be put to the test again, this time in a far distant realm of Magnamund. The nature of the quest and the perils that await you can be found in the next Grand Master adventure entitled:

THE DARKE CRUSADE

*XIV. Below is the South Gate of Kaag, its surface covered
by the hide of Nyxator.*

RANDOM NUMBER TABLE

8	7	6	1	3	1	6	8	6	2
0	8	6	5	0	5	8	7	4	1
9	5	1	2	5	7	4	3	1	8
5	2	4	7	6	5	8	6	0	9
0	1	9	5	4	9	0	3	1	4
5	8	1	4	3	6	7	2	8	5
9	8	6	7	8	0	2	3	4	0
6	2	0	3	4	1	8	6	2	9
8	4	8	7	6	5	2	1	0	6
4	2	5	2	9	0	5	4	8	7